P9-COP-230
POKÉMON™
POCKET COMICS
Legendary Pokémon
STORY & ART BY
SANTA HARUKAZE

CONTENTS

PART 1

PIKACHU'S SMILE HAS DISAPPEARED... SO OSHAWOTT AND FRIENDS ARE IN SEARCH OF THE LEGENDARY JOKE TO BRING IT BACK!

Ho-Hum Pikachu

MY FRIEND PIKACHU HASN'T BEEN SMILING RECENTLY...
grumph

Quiz Answer
?

I KNOW! THE BEST THING TO DO AT A TIME LIKE THIS...
...IS TO CRACK PIKACHU UP WITH MY BEST JOKES!

Starting with page 6, you'll find the answer to the quiz from the previous page here!

ta-dah
I'LL MOON PIKACHU... WITH A LUNAR POKÉMON!

grump grump
GUESS NOT...
twtch twtch

POKÉMON
QUIZ

Which of the following Pokémon is the exact same type as Pikachu?

1

Emolga

2

Magnemite

3

Mareep

Helpful Hoothoot

OSHAWOTT BEGINS BY ASKING HOOTHOOT FOR ADVICE.
YOU WANT TO MAKE PIKACHU LAUGH WITH A HILARIOUS JOKE ...?
SO...

Quiz answer for page 5.
3

ting
I KNOW WHERE TO FIND ONE—AND IT'S A *HOOT*!

Pikachu is only an Electric-type Pokémon, so Mareep is the correct answer. Emolga is an Electric- and Flying-type Pokémon. Magnemite is an Electric- and Steel-type Pokémon.

A HOOT?
IT'S A HOOT... GET IT?
WHAT'S THE JOKE...?
WELL, I THOUGHT THAT WAS HILARIOUS...

OH, GUESS WHAT...?
IT LOOKS LIKE I ONLY HAVE ONE TALON, BUT I ACTUALLY HAVE TWO! BET YOU DIDN'T KNOW THAT!
WILL YOU JUST HOP TO IT AND TELL ME YOUR JOKE?!
NOTE
HOOTHOOT SWITCHES FEET SO QUICKLY YOU CAN'T SEE IT.

POKéMON QUIZ

Which of the following Pokémon is heavier than Hoothoot?

1

Servine

2

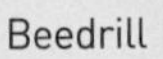

Beedrill

3

Xatu

Croagunk's Legendary Joke

I HEARD CROAGUNK KNOWS A REALLY FUNNY JOKE—IN FACT, IT'S LEGENDARY!
CROA-GUNK, WOULD YOU TELL ME YOUR JOKE?
fwp fwp fwp

Quiz answer for page 7.
2

HMM... YOU WANT ME TO TEACH YOU THE LEGENDARY JOKE, HUH?
I CAN'T TEACH IT TO YOU FOR FREE, YOU KNOW... ♡

Hoothoot is 46.7 lbs., Servine is 35.3 lbs. and Beedrill is 65.0 lbs. So Beedrill is the heaviest.

SHOOT ME WITH WATER GUN FIRST!
HUH ?!
UM... OKAY.

POKÉMON
QUIZ

Croagunk can have one of three different Abilities. One of them is Dry Skin. What are the other two?

1. Anticipation and Poison Touch
2. Tinted Lens and Reckless
3. Contrary and Rattled

WHEEEE! ♡
WATER GUN!!
THANKS! SAVES ME USING UP A POTION!
Sploosh
?
?
NOTE
POKÉMON WITH THE DRY SKIN ABILITY CAN HEAL THEIR HP WHEN ATTACKED WITH A WATER-TYPE MOVE.

Slipped My Mind

AH, THAT'S BETTER! FEELS GOOD TO BE MOIS-TURIZED!
NOW FOR THE JOKE...

Quiz answer for page 9.
1

YOU KNOW HOW TO USE AMNESIA, RIGHT...?
UM...

Croagunk's Abilities are Dry Skin, Anticipation and Poison Touch, which is a Hidden Ability.

POKéMON
QUIZ

POKÉMON WHO CAN LEARN AMNESIA
HEATMOR PANSEAR
WOOBAT BOUFFALANT
AUDINO LARVESTA
SCRAGGY ETC.
NO. I CAN'T LEARN AMNESIA.

OH, SORRY. I FORGOT!
HEY! COME BACK HERE!!
Maybe I'll remember next time!
Grrr!

How does Croagunk create the odd sounds that intimidate its opponents?

1. By stomping the ground with its feet
2. By inflating its poison sacs
3. By inflating its stomach

The Terrifying Legendary Joke

IT'LL MAKE YOU LAUGH UNTIL YOU FAINT!!
THIS NEXT JOKE IS DANGER-OUS!

Quiz answer for page 11.

2

HEH HEH... I SAID "FORGET" AGAIN. STILL WANNA HEAR IT?
IF YOU CAN'T USE AMNESIA... YOU CAN JUST FORGET ABOUT WAKING UP!!
I'M NOT FALLING FOR THAT AGAIN! FORGET I ASKED!

Croagunk inflates its poison sacs to create an eerie bubbling sound.

tmp
tmp

MOVES CROAGUNK CAN LEARN
FEINT ATTACK
SUCKER PUNCH
REVENGE
MUD BOMB
NASTY PLOT
ETC.
CROAGUNK CAN'T LEARN AMNESIA EITHER!!
WAIT A MINUTE...

POKÉMON
QUIZ

What is the correct effect of Amnesia? It...

1. ...increases the user's Special Defense by 2.
2. ...disables the opponent's last move.
3. ...resets the user's status conditions.

Oshawott's Journey Begins!

OSHAWOTT REALIZES CROAGUNK IS JUST TEASING HIM...
...AND DECIDES TO SET OUT THE NEXT DAY ON A QUEST FOR THE PERFECT JOKE.

Quiz answer for page 13.
1

THERE MUST BE A JOKE SOMEWHERE IN THIS WORLD THAT CAN BRING BACK PIKACHU'S SMILE!
THE LEGENDARY JOKE... IT'S UP TO ME TO FIND IT!

Amnesia raises the user's Special Defense by 2.

LOOK AT THAT...
TIME TO GET UP AND GO!
MORNING ALREADY!

IT WAS ACTUALLY JUST SOLROCK PEEKING INTO THE HOUSE.
WHAT ARE YOU UP TO, OSHA-WOTT?
NOTE
SOLROCK IS SAID TO COME FROM THE SUN. IT FLOATS IN MIDAIR AND MOVES SOUNDLESSLY.

POKÉMON
QUIZ

What category of Pokémon is Solrock?

1. Sun Pokémon
2. Unidentified Pokémon
3. Meteorite Pokémon

Super Sleuth Whismur

I'M WHISMUR, THE SUPER SLEUTH!
I CAN SOLVE ANY MYSTERY!

Quiz answer for page 15.
3

HUH?!
WHAT'S THIS? A SUSPICIOUS FOOTPRINT?!

Solrock is a Meteorite Pokémon.

LUCKILY I CAN IDENTIFY...
...WHO A FOOTPRINT BELONGS TO AT A GLANCE!
FOUR CLAWS
ROUND FOOT

IT WAS YOU, LOMBRE!
NOTE
LOMBRE HAS FOUR FINGERS (BUT NO CLAW ON ITS THUMB).

POKéMON QUIZ

Which Pokémon is the same weight as Whismur?

1

Palpitoad

2

Delibird

3

Lilligant

Prime Suspect

GUESS AGAIN, DETEC-TIVE.
MY FOOT IS SMALLER, AND THE SHAPE IS DIFFERENT TOO!
HMM... YOU'RE RIGHT...

Quiz answer for page 17.

3

Slam
OW ...?!

Whismur is 35.9 lbs., which is the same as Lilligant.

POKéMON
QUIZ

HUH?
NOTE
SUNKERN SUDDENLY DROPS OUT OF THE SKY.
LOOK...
SUNKERN...?!

How does Sunkern use its leaves to drive away its enemies? By...

1. ...shaking them.
2. ...emitting a stench from them.
3. ...throwing them at its enemy.

YEP!
IT WAS ME. LESS OF A FOOTPRINT AND MORE OF A FACE-PLANT.
AHA! *YOU'RE* THE CULPRIT!

A... What?

I'M NOT A CULPRIT...
I'M A GRASS TYPE.
UM...

Quiz answer for page 19.
1

YEAH
...

Sunkern shakes its leaves frantically to defend itself from its enemies.

fwump
OBVI-
OUSLY...
...THEY'RE
IN
CAHOOTS!

ZiiiPPP
CAHOOTS
?!
WHAT'S A
CAHOOT?
I'M SUPER
SLEUTH
WHISMUR...
ALWAYS ON
THE GO!

POKÉMON
QUIZ

What does Lombre eat?

1 Waterweeds from lakes

2 Aquatic moss from riverbeds

3 Shellfish from beaches

Search for Shelmet

I AM SUPER SLEUTH WHISMUR!
YOU WANT ME TO FIND SHELMET?
NOTE
KARRABLAST AND SHELMET NEED EACH OTHER TO EVOLVE.

Quiz answer for page 21.
2

I SEARCHED FOR THREE DAYS AND NIGHTS!!
QUESTIONING
CAMPING OUT
LEAVE IT TO A PROFES-SIONAL!

Lombre feeds off aquatic moss that grows on rocks in riverbeds.

AND FINALLY, I FOUND IT!
OOH!!

NOW THEN... ABOUT MY FEE...
WE HAVE NO IDEA WHAT YOU'RE TALKING ABOUT.
WE JUST GOT HERE.
DIDN'T WE, ESCAVA-LIER?
We sure did, Accel-gor!
NOTE
THESE TWO EVOLVE TOGETHER WHEN STIMULATED BY AN ELECTRIC SHOCK.

POKéMON QUIZ

Which one is heavier, Karrablast or Shelmet?

1

Karrablast

2

Shelmet

3

They weigh the same.

MINI-BREAK 1

Basculin

I WANT TO BEAT UP THE RED BASCULIN...
...BUT I'M LAUGHING TOO MUCH AT THESE JOKES!!
NOTE
RED AND BLUE BASCULIN DON'T GET ALONG. THEY ARE VERY HOSTILE POKÉMON.

Quiz answer for page 23.

2

Karrablast is 13.0 lbs. and Shelmet is 17.0 lbs., so Shelmet is heavier.

A GROUP OF SANDILE IN THE DESERT...
...IS AN O-EYE-SIS!
NOTE
SANDILE LIVE BURIED IN THE SANDS OF THE DESERT.

MINI-BREAK 1

Sandile

MINI-
BREAK
1

Meditite

"YO-YOGA"...
...IS THE WORD FOR MEDITATIVE POSES PERFORMED WHILE FLOATING UP AND DOWN.
NOTE
MEDITITE FLOATS IN THE AIR WHEN MEDITATING TO HEIGHTEN ITS INNER ENERGY.

MINI-BREAK 1

Whose Tail?

Which Pokémon on the right matches which tail on the left? See if you can connect them all!

MINI-
BREAK
1

Arceus

Quiz answer
for page 27.

?

THERE ARE SO MANY TYPES OF ARCEUS...
...THEY EVEN CONFUSE THEMSELVES!
NOTE
THE BODY COLOR OF AN ARCEUS CHANGES WHEN IT CHANGES ITS POKÉMON TYPE.

The answer is
on page 252.

BENDY TONGUES...
...FOR WHEN YOU ABSOLUTELY, POSITIVELY HAVE TO SNEAK UP ON THAT APPLE!
NOTE
PALPITOAD USES ITS LONG STICKY TONGUE TO CAPTURE ITS PREY.

MINI-BREAK 1

Palpitoad

MINI-BREAK
1

Cofagrigus

LILLIGANT LIKES MUMS... NOT MUMMIES.

No !!

gah

NOTE

COFAGRIGUS'S MOVE GRUDGE CAUSES ITS OPPONENT TO LOSE ALL THE PP OF THE ATTACK MOVE THAT MADE IT FAINT.

Which Pokémon?

Which Pokémon on the right matches which description on the left? See if you can connect them all!

The Walking Jungle

The Kick Master

The Summoner of Night

The Desert Spirit

A Tough Case

I AM SUPER SLEUTH WHISMUR.
HI.
I RECEIVED A UNIQUE REQUEST TODAY.

Quiz answer for page 31.

?

The answer is on page 252.

YOU'RE SEARCHING FOR THE LEGENDARY JOKE?!
THAT'S A NUTTY CASE!!

POKéMON
QUIZ

...IT'LL BE HARD TO CRACK. ♡
MEANING...
heh heh...

THAT WAS A TERRIBLE JOKE.
WAIT, I'M SORRY! NO MORE PUNS, I PROMISE!
drag drag drag
I'M SUPER SLEUTH WHISMUR... AND I NEVER LET GO OF A CASE UNTIL IT'S SOLVED!

When does Whismur stop crying at an earsplitting volume? When...

1. ...it closes its eyes.
2. ...its ears are shut.
3. ...it's tired.

Contacts

A SLEUTH HAS A WIDE NETWORK OF CONTACTS TO DRAW ON FOR INTEL.

I KNOW JUST WHO TO ASK!

MY FRIEND UXIE...
UXIE
A POKÉ-MON KNOWN AS...
...THE BEING OF KNOWLEDGE.
UXIE IS SURE TO HAVE A CLUE!

Quiz answer for page 33.

2

Whismur will stop crying when its ears are shut.

Pokémon
QUIZ

HURRY, SO WE CAN LEARN THE LEGENDARY JOKE!
DON'T RUN, WHISMUR!
fooosh

I'M A SLOW LEARNER...
trip

Which of the following three statements is true of Uxie? It...

1. ...sleeps at the bottom of a lake.
2. ...can erase the memory of whoever looks into its eyes.
3. ...sings the Relic Song during battle.

Search for the Legendary Joke

HI, WHISMUR...
CAN I HELP YOU?
WE'RE SEARCH-ING FOR THE LEGEND-ARY JOKE!

LEGENDARY, HUH? WELL, I AM A LEGENDARY POKÉMON...
I WONDER IF THAT HAS SOMETHING TO DO WITH IT?
NOTE
IN ADDITION TO UXIE, AZELF AND MESPRIT ARE ALSO LEGENDARY POKÉMON.

Quiz answer for page 35.

2

Uxie erases the memory of whoever gazes into its eyes.

REALLY?! YOU ARE?!
BUT... I DON'T. YOU'LL HAVE TO ASK THE OTHERS.
OF COURSE! A LEGENDARY POKÉMON MUST KNOW THE LEGENDARY JOKE!!

ONLY ABOUT 30 OR SO...
DON'T WORRY... THERE AREN'T THAT MANY LEGENDARY POKÉMON.
ONLY 30...?!
NOTE
CURRENTLY, THERE ARE MORE THAN 35 LEGENDARY POKÉMON.

POKÉMON
QUIZ

Which of the following is a Legendary Pokémon?

1. 
Charizard

2. 
Togekiss

3. 
Moltres

Search for the Legendary Pokémon

WHAT NOW?
HOW ARE WE GOING TO FIND THE RIGHT LEGENDARY POKÉMON?
DON'T WORRY.

Quiz answer for page 37.
3

IT MIGHT SURPRISE YOU, BUT... I HAVE A REALLY LOUD VOICE!
WE JUST NEED THEM TO FIND US!
NOTE
WHISMUR'S CRY IS AS LOUD AS A JET PLANE.

Moltres is a Legendary Fire- and Flying-type Pokémon.

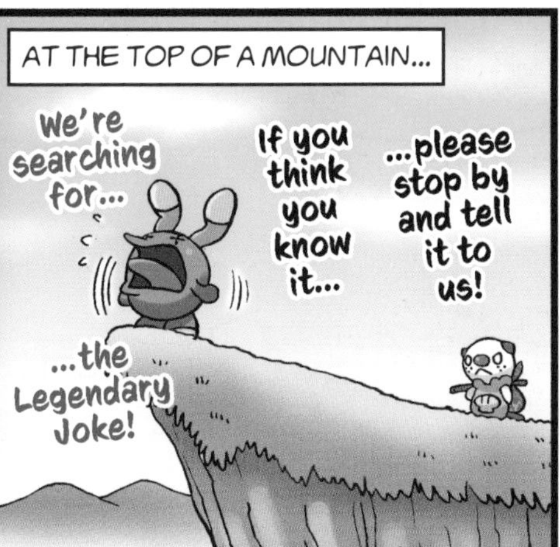

AT THE TOP OF A MOUNTAIN...
We're searching for...
...the Legendary Joke!
If you think you know it...
...please stop by and tell it to us!

QUIET!
YOU'LL WAKE THE BABY!!
NOTE
KANGASKHAN RAISES ITS BABY IN ITS POUCH.

POKÉMON QUIZ

How does Kangaskhan sleep to avoid squishing its baby?

1. Sitting down
2. Standing up
3. On its back

Misunder-standings

I THINK WE OUGHT TO KEEP OUR VOICES DOWN...
...SO WE DON'T DISTURB OUR NEIGHBORS.
OWW...
twitch twitch
YOU THINK ...?

Quiz answer for page 39.
1

HEY, DID YOU CALL FOR ME...?

Kangaskhan sleeps sitting down.

NOTE
TIMBURR OFTEN APPEARS WITH A PIECE OF LUMBER TO HELP OUT WITH CONSTRUCTION PROJECTS.
HERE I AM!

DID SOMEONE SAY "LEGENDARY LOG"?
...WE SAID "LEGENDARY JOKE." AND HOW IS THAT LOG LEGENDARY ANYWAY?
NO...
topple

POKÉMON QUIZ

Which of the following is not true about Timburr and its lumber?

1. It swings its log around to fight.
2. It builds itself a log house.
3. It carries bigger logs when it grows larger.

More Misunderstandings

WE SAID "STOP BY" NOT "ELECTRIFY"...
krcki krcki
NOTE
GALVANTULA CREATES ELECTRICALLY CHARGED WEBS TO TRAP ITS PREY.

Quiz answer for page 41.

2

Timburr doesn't build itself a log house.

WE SAID "THINK" NOT "LINK"...
We're linked together!
NOTE
MAGNETON IS A POKÉMON FORMED BY THREE MAGNEMITE LINKED TOGETHER.

WE SAID "KNOW" NOT "SNOW"...
whoooosh
NOTE
ABOMASNOW CREATES BLIZZARDS.

POKéMON
QUIZ

How does Galvantula use its electrified web to defend itself?

1. It wraps its web around its enemy.
2. It creates an electric barrier.
3. It crumples its web into a ball and throws it.

DO I MUMBLE WHEN I SHOUT...?!
THANKS ANYWAY THOUGH...
hurumph
razzle frazzle

Legendary Cobalion

Quiz answer for page 43.

2

Galvantula creates an electric barrier to protect itself and stun its opponent.

glare...
NOTE
EVEN THE MOST HOSTILE POKÉMON OBEY COBALION WHEN IT STARES THEM DOWN.

UM...
ting

WOULD YOU LIKE A SEAT?
nod

...AND THAT'S WHY...
...COBALION HAS NEVER LOST A GAME OF MUSICAL CHAIRS!
Huh?!
WOW!!

POKéMON
QUIZ

Which of the three Pokémon below is the tallest?

1

Cobalion

2

Terrakion

3

Virizion

Legendary Virizion

Quiz answer for page 45.
1

Cobalion is 6'11", Terrakion is 6'03" and Virizion is 6'07". So Cobalion is the tallest.

NOTE
THE HORNS ON VIRIZION'S HEAD ARE AS SHARP AS BLADES.

Aaaaaah!
I WAS TAKING A WALK...
...WHEN OUT OF THE BLUE, VIRIZION PASSED BY!
WHERE IS YOUR HEAD, SQUIRTLE ?!
Stggr
Stggr

HUH ...?
POP
RIGHT HERE. IT WAS JUST IN MY SHELL.
Phew!

POKéMON
QUIZ

Which of the three Pokémon below is the lightest?

WE THOUGHT YOU'D TANGLED WITH VIRIZION...
Virizion's blades are really sharp, you know...
Brr! That was scary!

1

Cobalion

2

Terrakion

3

Virizion

Legendary Terrakion

NOTE
TERRAKION IS SO POWERFUL IT CAN BREAK THROUGH A GIANT CASTLE WALL.

Quiz answer for page 47.
3

Weighing in at 440.9 lbs., Virizion is the lightest.

THROH DECIDED TO TRY A LITTLE HEAD-TO-HEAD TRAINING WITH TERRAKION...
Oh yeah!

POKÉMON
QUIZ

Aaaaahhh!
ka-whump
OH MY...
THEN WHAT HAPPENED...?!
THROH GOT KNOCKED SKY-HIGH, AND...

aa a a a a h!
AND IT'S STILL UP THERE!
NO WAY ...

Which of the following is Terrakion's Ability?

1 Steadfast

2 Prankster

3 Justified

Three Legendary Pokémon

AND THAT'S ALL...
...THE INTEL I FOUND ON COBALION, VIRIZION AND TERRAKION.
IT'S NOT VERY USEFUL...

Quiz answer for page 49.

3

VIRIZION LIVES IN A FOREST... SO LET'S LOOK FOR IT THERE!
AT ANY RATE... THERE'S A FOREST AHEAD OF US!

Cobalion, Virizion and Terrakion all have the Justified Ability.

...FOON-
GUS!
HEY...
Huh?!

HOW COULD YOU TELL I WASN'T A WILD POKÉ BALL?
I WAS PERFECTLY CAMOU-FLAGED!!

NOTE

NO ONE KNOWS WHY FOONGUS RESEMBLES A POKÉ BALL.

POKéMON
QUIZ

Which Pokémon is the same height as Foongus?

1

Budew

2

Gothita

3

Rattata

MINI-BREAK 2

Zebstrika

Quiz answer for page 51.
1

Foongus is 0'08" and so is Budew.

TONGUE TWISTER
FEMALE ZEBSTRIKA BLITZLE BABY STRIKES ZEALOUSLY... (REPEAT AS FAST AS YOU CAN!)
NOTE
ZEBSTRIKA IS A VERY ILL-TEMPERED POKÉMON.

MINI-BREAK 2

Leavanny

TONGUE TWISTER

MALE LEAVANNY
DADDY'S
BUG-TYPE
GRASS-TYPE
BABY
WEAVES
LEAVES
WELL...
(REPEAT
QUICKLY!)

NOTE

LEAVANNY WEAVES CLOTHES FOR SMALL POKÉMON.

MINI-
BREAK
2

Alomomola

TONGUE TWISTER

MALE ALOMOMOLA
PAPA ALOMOMOLA
LOVES FEMALE
ALOMOMOLA MAMA
ALOMOMOLA
LOVINGLY.

NOTE

THE MEMBRANE ENVELOPING ALOMOMOLA'S BODY HAS THE ABILITY TO HEAL WOUNDS.

MINI-BREAK 2

Lickitung

...Papa Alomo...
Ouch!
OW, OW... I BIT MY TONGUE!
NO, YOU DIDN'T. YOU DON'T HAVE ANY TEETH.

OH...
IT DOESN'T HURT!
YEP...
You're right...
YOU DON'T HAVE TO WORRY ABOUT BITING YOUR TONGUE DOING TONGUE TWIST-ERS!

MINI-
BREAK
2

Luxio

ELECTRICITY GIVES YOU A SPARKLING PERSONALITY.
GET IT?
Like me!
NOTE
POWERFUL ELECTRIC CURRENTS COURSE THROUGH THE TIP OF LUXIO'S CLAWS.
You're not sparking my interest...
NOTE
BANETTE IS A DISCARDED DOLL WHO TURNED INTO A POKÉMON OUT OF BITTERNESS AFTER BEING THROWN AWAY.

Which Pokémon?

Which Pokémon on the right matches which category on the left? See if you can connect them all!

Sun Pokémon

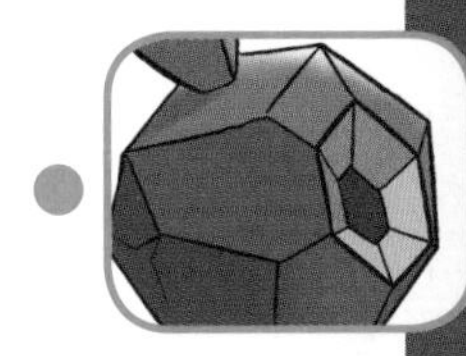

Meteorite Pokémon

Temporal Pokémon

Mantle Pokémon

Dangers of the Night Forest

YOU KNOW, YOU SHOULDN'T EVEN THINK ABOUT...
...ENTERING THE FOREST AT NIGHT!

Quiz answer for page 57.

?

The answer is on page 253.

IT'S VERY DANGER-OUS AFTER DARK!
PITCH-BLACK TOO...
NO PROBLEM!

I'LL HELP YOU FIND YOUR WAY THROUGH THE DARKNESS!
Hello!
WHO ARE YOU?

I'M WATCHOG.
LEAVE EVERY-THING TO ME! ♡
NOTE
WATCHOG CAN SEE IN THE DARK!

POKéMON QUIZ

What does Watchog do when it sees an enemy?

1. Performs a handstand
2. Raises its tail up high
3. Crouches down

Glowing in the Dark

WHOA...
IT REALLY IS PITCH-BLACK INSIDE THE FOREST AT NIGHT.
DON'T WORRY. ♡

Quiz answer for page 59.

2

YOU CAN SEE ME IN THE DARK, CAN'T YOU...?
JUST FOLLOW ME.
gleam
NOTE
THE PATTERN ON WATCHOG'S BODY GLOWS IN THE DARK.

Watchog raises its tail up high when it spots an enemy.

Smak
What the—?!

DID YOU BUMP INTO SOME-THING?
BEING ABLE TO SEE IN THE DARK ISN'T VERY HELPFUL IF YOU DON'T LOOK WHERE YOU'RE GOING!

What does Watchog store inside its cheek pouches?

1. Berries
2. Berry seeds
3. Berry skins

What's in the Bag?

THAT BAG ON YOUR SHOUL-DER...
HEY, OSHA-WOTT...
WHAT'S INSIDE IT?

Quiz answer for page 61.

2

WHY DO YOU ASK?
OH, NO REASON...

Watchog attacks its enemies with the seeds of berries it stores in its cheek pouches.

OSHAWOTT...
I DON'T TRUST WATCHOG.
I THINK IT'S AFTER YOUR BAG...

WANT ME TO CARRY YOUR BAG FOR YOU?
glance
IT MUST BE REALLY HEAVY...

POKéMON
QUIZ

Which Pokémon carries things for people?

1

Bibarel

2

Bayleef

3

Machoke

Escape in the Dark

HUH?
ZOOM

Quiz answer for page 63.

3

HEY! WHERE ARE YOU GOING?!
DON'T GO THAT WAY! IT'S DANGER-OUS!!

Machoke happily carries heavy cargo for others to build up its strength.

I CAN'T SEE A THING IN THE DARK!!
hff
hff
hff
hff
BUT WE HAVE TO GET AWAY FROM WATCHOG!

krckl
LOOK!
SOME-THING'S SHINING OVER THERE...

Which of the following Pokémon can see in the dark?

1

Steelix

2

Darumaka

3

Pupitar

A New Guide

I'D BE HAPPY TO SHOW YOU THE WAY IF YOU LIKE.
glow glow
GOOD EVENING...
NOTE
LITWICK OFFERS TO GUIDE OTHERS SO ITS FLAME CAN ABSORB THEIR LIFE-FORCE.

Quiz answer for page 65.
1

ARE YOU NOW?
WELL, JUST FOLLOW ME!
WE'RE SEARCHING FOR A LEGENDARY POKÉMON.
UM...
THANKS A LOT!

Steelix can travel underground because it can see in the dark.

KEEP AN EYE ON MY FLAME...
...AND FOLLOW ME CLOSELY... AND QUIETLY...
glow
glow

POKéMON
QUIZ

Litwick absorbs the life-force of Pokémon and people. What category is it?

OSHAWOTT...
STARING AT THAT FLAME IS MAKING ME SICK.
Me too...
BUT HOW ELSE ARE WE GOING TO GET THROUGH THESE WOODS?

1. Light Pokémon
2. Spitfire Pokémon
3. Candle Pokémon

Saved by a Bug Behind

Huh ?
Hey ...!
THEY WERE SO QUIET I DIDN'T NOTICE THAT I LOST THEM!
wfff

Quiz answer for page 67.

3

I SEEM TO HAVE FOLLOWED A DIFFER-ENT LIGHT.
WAIT... I DON'T THINK THIS IS RIGHT, WHISMUR!
Huh ?

Litwick is a Candle Pokémon.

EXCUSE ME...!
Quit staring at my behind!
UGH... I FEEL DIZZY.
shff
Wbbl
Wbbl

POKéMON
QUIZ

How many different patterns can Illumise draw in the sky using Volbeat? More than...

1 ...100.

2 ...200.

3 ...300.

YOU'RE LUCKY YOU GOT SEPARATED. LITWICK'S FLAME ABSORBS THE LIFE-FORCE OF PEOPLE AND POKÉMON, YOU KNOW...
YOU MUST HAVE MET LITWICK.
Oh...
PHEW! GOOD THING THAT'S BEHIND US NOW AND WE'RE BEHIND YOUR...BEHIND. OOPS... SORRY.

Are You Dangerous Too?

WOW...
THE FOREST IS SO DAN-GEROUS AT NIGHT...
ARE YOU A DANGER-OUS POKÉMON TOO?
WHO, ME?!

Quiz answer for page 69.

2

I'M AN ADORABLE BUG-TYPE POKÉMON!
I NEVER HURT ANY-ONE!
THAT'S A RELIEF. ♡
Phew...
HEY, DO YOU KNOW ANYTHING ABOUT LEGENDARY POKÉMON?

Over 200 different patterns have been confirmed so far.

YOU WANT ME TO CALL IT FOR YOU?
THE ONLY ONE I'VE SEEN AROUND HERE IS VIRIZION.
REALLY?
WHISMUR! REMEMBER TO KEEP IT DOWN!

POKÉMON QUIZ

What is Volbeat's Habitat?

1. Clean ponds
2. Clean rivers
3. Mountains with beautiful views

...VOLBEAT!
LEAVE IT TO US...
BZZZZBZZZZ
NOTE
VOLBEAT IS ATTRACTED BY THE SWEET AROMA OF ILLUMISE AND DRAWS SHAPES IN THE NIGHT SKY WITH ITS GLOWING TAIL.

Helpful Volbeat

Quiz answer for page 71.

1

VIRIZION!

Volbeat lives around clean ponds.

COME HERE!

POKÉMON
QUIZ

Which of the Pokémon below is not a Legendary Pokémon?

1

Entei

2

Articuno

3

Munchlax

Arrival of a Legendary

UH-HUH. I AGREE.
I'M SCARED. MAYBE WE SHOULD JUST MAKE A RUN FOR IT...

Quiz answer for page 73.
3

TOO LATE!!
AIIEEE!
VIRIZION?!
Eeeeek!

Munchlax is not a Legendary Pokémon.

A JOKE! I'LL LIGHTEN THE MOOD WITH A COMBO PUN AND COMPLIMENT! UMM...
I BET YOU LOOK LOVELY AT THE EDGE OF THE PLANET!
MY NAME'S "VIRIZION," NOT "HORIZON."

WE DIDN'T CALL YOU HERE FOR A POKÉMON BATTLE...
WE JUST WANT TO TALK TO YOU...
OH. SORRY.

POKÉMON
QUIZ

Virizion attacks with Magical Leaf. Which of the following Pokémon is it super effective against?

1

Taillow

2

Nidoking

3

Typhlosion

Teach Us the Legendary Joke

WE WANT YOU TO TEACH US THE LEG-ENDARY JOKE!!
SO WHAT DO YOU WANT FROM ME...?!

Quiz answer for page 75.

2

THAT LEAVES COBALION AND TERRAKION THEN...
OKAY ...
HUH?
THE... WHAT?
Never heard of it.

Magical Leaf is super effective against Nidoking, because it is a Poison- and Ground-type Pokémon.

WOULD YOU HAPPEN TO KNOW WHERE THEY ARE?
HM...
COBALION IS PROBABLY IN THAT CAVE...
NOTE
YOU CAN MEET COBALION BY USING SURF AT ROUTE 6 TO REACH MISTRALTON CAVE.

POKéMON QUIZ

Cobalion is calm and collected. They say Cobalion has...

1 ...a heart of steel.

2 ...a body of steel.

3 ...a heart and body of steel.

AT THE BREAK OF DAY, THE THREE HEAD FOR THE CAVE...
YOU CAN FOLLOW ME IF YOU LIKE...

Just Dropping By

THERE'S THE CAVE.
AND COBALION IS INSIDE IT?!

HEY, COBALION!!
...

Quiz answer for page 77.

3

It's said that Cobalion has a heart and body of steel.

ARE YOU SURE IT'S INSIDE THIS CAVE?
Of course.

HEY! THIS VISIT IS FOR A *JUST* CAUSE! SO WOULD YOU *JUST* COME OUT FOR A SEC?
YOU CALLED ...?
POP
NOTE
COBALION'S ABILITY IS JUSTIFIED.

POKÉMON QUIZ

Which of the following Pokémon can have the Justified Ability?

1

Ledian

2

Dewott

3

Gallade

The Quest for Terrakion Begins

NEVER HEARD OF IT... BUT TERRAKION MIGHT HAVE.
THE LEGENDARY JOKE?

Quiz answer for page 79.

3

I CAN TELL YOU WHICH WAY TERRAKION WENT, IF YOU WANT.
YOU CAN?!

Gallade's Hidden Ability is Justified.

IT SMASHED THROUGH THOSE WALLS...
JUST KEEP GOING IN THAT DIRECTION...
THATA-WAY...
NOTE
TERRAKION'S CHARGE IS STRONG ENOUGH TO BREAK THROUGH STONE WALLS.

...ALL WE HAVE TO DO IS FOLLOW ITS TRAIL DOWN THIS PATH.
VIRIZION, COBALION, AND NOW...
THANKS!
TELL TERRAKION "HELLO" FOR US!

POKéMON QUIZ

Which of the following Pokémon is famous for its powerful charges?

1

Sceptile

2

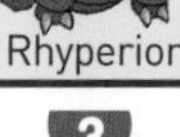
Rhyperior

3

Bouffalant

Helpful Pansage

WHISMUR AND OSHAWOTT WALK FOR A LONG TIME...

AT LEAST IT'S EASY TO TELL...

...WHICH WAY IT WENT.

Quiz answer for page 81.
3

ALONG THE WAY, OUR FRIENDS MEET ALL SORTS OF POKÉMON.
PANSAGE
HIYA! ARE YOU ON A JOURNEY?

Bouffalant's headbutt is powerful enough to derail a train.

IF YOU'RE TIRED FROM ALL THAT WALKING...
...YOU SHOULD EAT ONE OF MY LEAVES. ♡
ARE YOU TIRED, OSHA-WOTT?
NOTE
EATING A LEAF FROM PANSAGE'S HEAD WHISKS AWAY YOUR WEARINESS LIKE MAGIC.

POKÉMON
QUIZ

What is Pansage good at?

1. Finding berries
2. Finding enemies
3. Singing

NO, THANKS. UNTIL PIKACHU SMILES AGAIN...
...I DON'T HAVE TIME TO GET TIRED!
...

Offer Not Accepted

I'VE MADE UP MY MIND...
I'M GOING TO SOLVE THIS CASE NO MATTER WHAT IT TAKES!
Hey ...

Quiz answer for page 83.
1

ARE YOU SURE?
DON'T YOU WANT A LEAF SNACK?
THEY'RE REALLY TASTY, YOU KNOW!

Pansage is good at finding berries. It shares them with its friends.

AREN'T YOU HUNGRY?
I'M GOOD FOR NOW. I HAVE TRAIL MIX.
What...? Seriously?

POKéMON QUIZ

Where does Pansage live?

1 Fields

2 Towns

3 Forests

Sniff!
Sniff!
BUT EVERY-ONE LOVES MY LEAVES!!

The Nosepass Knows...

OUR FRIENDS MEET NOSE-PASS...
SOME-BODY STOP ME!!
Wff
Wff
Wff

Quiz answer for page 85.

3

SOME-THING BUMPED INTO ME...
WHY ARE YOU SPIN-NING AROUND LIKE THAT?!
smak
urrrk
IT MUST HAVE BEEN TERRAK-ION!

Pansage lives deep in the forest.

YOU STOPPED MY SPINNING!
THANK YOU!

UM... WE'RE OVER HERE.
NOTE
NOSEPASS'S NOSE ALWAYS POINTS NORTH.
I KNOW.
North

POKéMON
QUIZ

Nosepass's body emits a strong magnetic field that is...

1 ...always the same.

2 ...stronger in cold seasons.

3 ...stronger in hot seasons.

Drubbed Durant

OUR FRIENDS MEET DURANT.
HEY THERE!
ARE YOU FRIENDS WITH THAT POKÉMON WHO JUST WENT BY?!

Quiz answer for page 87.
2

YOU'RE ALL TALK-ING AT ONCE!
I CAN'T UNDER-STAND YOU...
murmur murmur murmur murmur murmur

The colder it is, the stronger Nosepass's magnetism becomes.

NOTE
DURANT MOVE WELL TOGETHER AS A GROUP.
We Got trampled
shffl shffl

GREAT. DO I NEED A LAWYER OR AN EXTERMINATOR?
We're going to sue
shffl shffl

POKéMON
QUIZ

Which of the following Pokémon is Durant's natural predator?

1

Heatmor

2

Pawniard

3

Golett

Pokémon in Trouble

Quiz answer for page 89.

1

WHIMSICOTT IS STUCK IN A TREE...
NOTE
WHIMSICOTT APPEARS ALONG WITH WHIRLWINDS.
CAN I GET A LITTLE HELP HERE ...?

FERROSEED GOT SMASHED INTO A ROCK...
mumbl mumbl
NOTE
FERROSEED SHOOTS BARRAGES OF SPIKES WHEN IT'S THREAT-ENED. (BUT IN THIS CASE, THERE WASN'T ENOUGH TIME...)

Durant's natural predator is Heatmor.

IT LOOKS LIKE...
...TERAKKION IS CAUSING PROBLEMS...
...FOR EVERYONE.

FINALLY, WE MEET!!
krunch
!
BUT BEFORE WE GET TO THAT...

POKéMON
QUIZ

What category of Pokémon is Whimsicott?

1. Cyclone Pokémon
2. Wind Chime Pokémon
3. Windveiled Pokémon

And Now, the News!

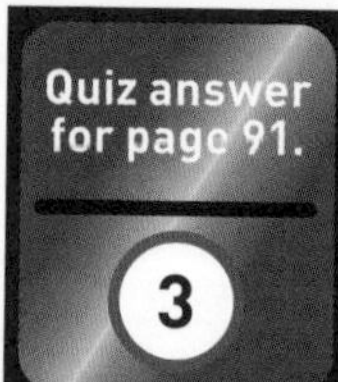

Quiz answer for page 91.
3

Whimsicott is a Windveiled Pokémon.

GENIUS ME-OWTH'S...
NEWS SHOW
...NEWS SHOW !!
Oh Yeah!
FIRST UP, A STORY ABOUT...
...THE IN-CREDIBLE THIEF PURR-LOIN!
NOTE
PEOPLE FORGIVE PURRLOIN FOR STEALING THEIR THINGS BECAUSE IT'S JUST SO DARN CUTE!

SOMETIMES IT STEALS THINGS IT DOESN'T INTEND TO!
UM...

See you later, cutie!
You stole my heart!
Jynx
Eeek!
CONGRATU-LATIONS, PURRLOIN!

POKÉMON QUIZ

What is Purrloin's Pokémon type?

1 Dark type

2 Normal type

3 Poison type

World Travelers

TORNADUS FLIES AT 200 MILES PER HOUR.
OH YEAH! I WENT ALL THE WAY AROUND THE WORLD!
WZZZZ...
Starting point

Quiz answer for page 93.

1

I CAN DO THAT TOO!
PIECE OF CAKE... ♡
Ha ha ha...
Watch!
NOTE
MIME JR. MIMICS THE EXPRESSIONS AND MOTIONS OF OTHERS.

Purrloin is a Dark-type Pokémon.

La
La
La
La
...

WHAT ARE YOU DOING?!
I JUST WENT AROUND THE WORLD! WHEE!
I DIDN'T GET IT QUITE RIGHT, DID I...?

POKéMON QUIZ

How fast can Tornadus fly?

1. 100 mph
2. 200 mph
3. 300 mph

Zweilous Goes Head-to-Head

ZWEILOUS GOT INTO A FIGHT... WITH ITSELF!
I LOST BECAUSE OF YOU!!
WHAT?! NO, I LOST BECAUSE OF YOU!!
NOTE
ZWEILOUS'S TWO HEADS DON'T GET ALONG.

Quiz answer for page 95.
2

HEY! YOU OVER THERE...!
WHICH ONE OF US LOST?
UM...
L-LOST... WHAT?

Tornadus can fly at speeds of 200 mph.

OKAY, OKAY... YOU LOST.
HUH ...?!
Ha ha ha ha
TOLD-JA!
WHY ?!
JUST A HUNCH.
I WAS RIGHT! NYAH NYAH NYAH NYAH NYAH! ♡

GLAD TO BE OF HELP.
Landorus was wrong! And I'm not moving until you admit it!
Well I'm not moving until you admit I'm right!!
wfff
BOTH SIDES ARE GOING TO BE THERE FOR A WHILE...

What will Zweilous evolve into?

1

Hydreigon

2

Volcarona

3

Scolipede

To Each Its Own

TRUBBISH SAYS IT'S LOST SOMETHING...
...PRE-CIOUS.
SNFFL SNFFL

Quiz answer for page 97.
1

Zweilous evolves into Hydreigon.

I WAS SO LOOKING FOR-WARD...
...TO EATING IT!!

EATING WHAT ...?
A SMELLY, ROTTEN, SQUISHED-UP BERRY!
NOTE
TRUBBISH FOLLOWS LITTERERS TO GATHER THEIR GARBAGE.

POKéMON QUIZ

Where does Trubbish dwell?

1. Unsanitary places
2. Crowded places
3. Caves

ROTTEN FOOD TASTES SO MUCH BETTER THAN FRESH FOOD!
UM... I'M NO GOURMET COOK, BUT...
...garbage is still garbage!

On the Road

AN ACCIDENT HAS JUST BEEN REPORTED!
LET'S HEAD TO THE SCENE!

Quiz answer for page 99.
1

twtch
twtch
HUH?

Trubbish loves unsanitary places.

JUST TWO UNCON-SCIOUS POKÉMON WITH BUMPS ON THEIR HEADS.
THERE'S NO ACCI-DENT HERE.
THAT'S WHAT HAPPENS WHEN...

POKÉMON QUIZ

What does Larvitar feed on?

1. Fallen leaves
2. Flower nectar
3. Soil

...YOU TRY TO RUN THROUGH UNDER-GROUND TUNNELS... IN THE DARK!
?
?
?

Lilligant's Recital

TALENTED LILLIGANT...
...IS PER-FORMING A RECITAL FOR US TODAY!
THANK YOU SO MUCH FOR COMING. ♡

Quiz answer for page 101.

3

NOTE
IT IS A CHALLENGE FOR EVEN A VETERAN TRAINER TO GET LILLIGANT TO BLOOM ITS BEAUTIFUL FLOWER.
WOOHOOO!
IS IT A NEW DANCE ?!
WHAT KIND OF A PERFOR-MANCE IS THIS ?!
IS IT A NEW SONG ?!

Larvitar feeds on the soil around it.

READY ...?!

IT'S JUST A GAME OF PEEKA-BOO?!
wfff
PEEKA-BOO!!

POKéMON
QUIZ

When you smell the garland on Lilligant's head you feel...

1 ...refreshed.

2 ...relaxed.

3 ...invigorated and ready for battle.

The Amazing Darmanitan!

Hyyuuu...
AT THE MOMENT, DAR-MANITAN IS...
...LOCKED IN A SERIOUS MENTAL BATTLE!
NOTE
DARMANITAN TRANSFORMS INTO A STONE STATUE WHEN IT IS WEAKENED IN BATTLE.

Quiz answer for page 103.
2

SO...WHO ARE YOU FIGHTING NOW?
THE QUES-TION ISN'T ***WHO***...

The fragrance of the garland on Lilligant's head has a relaxing effect.

POKéMON
QUIZ

MY BACK ITCHES...
...BUT WHAT!
UM...
WANT ME TO SCRATCH IT FOR YOU...?
ITCH
ITCH

NO! I GOT THIS! FOCUS... FOCUS...
urmph
UHH...
GUESS EVERYONE HAS THEIR OWN BATTLES TO FIGHT...

When Darmanitan is in Zen Mode, it fights with its mind. In what other way does Darmanitan change when it is in Zen Mode?

1. Its weight becomes 220 lbs.
2. Its speed is halved.
3. It becomes a Fire- and Psychic-type Pokémon.

Take Me to Your Leader

A NEW LEADER HAS BEEN CHOSEN...
...IN SCRAFTY'S TOWN.
Eyep

Quiz answer for page 105.

3

NOTE
THE SCRAFTY WITH THE BIGGEST CREST BECOMES THEIR LEADER.
CREST
PROVING THAT MY CREST IS THE BIGGEST...

Darmanitan changes from a Fire-type Pokémon to a Fire- and Psychic-type Pokémon.

OOOOO
BIGGER CREST

SO THEY SWAP PLACES...
LEADER!! LEADER!!
Who...
...me?!
NEW LEADER!! NEW LEADER!!
Yayyy
I hope you're a better camera operator than you are a leader.

POKéMON QUIZ

What does a group of Scrafty do to an intruder who trespasses on their territory?

1. Beat it up
2. Battle it in a one-on-one battle
3. Ignore it

Searching for a Scoop

THERE ARE NO GOOD NEWS STORIES HERE.
SIGH...

Quiz answer for page 107.

1

A group of Scrafty will beat up anyone who enters their territory.

HEY, WHAT ARE YOU DOING HERE?
WE WERE JUST TAKING A LITTLE BREAK.
WE'RE ON A QUEST FOR THE LEGEND-ARY JOKE!

I FOUND MY STORY!!
GET THE CAM-ERA!!
C-camera...?
ARE YOU ROLLING?!

POKÉMON
QUIZ

What type of Pokémon is Meowth?

1. Psychic type
2. Normal type
3. Dark type

The Legendary ...Scoop?

YOU'RE ON A JOURNEY TO BRING A SMILE TO YOUR FRIEND'S FACE...?
TO FIND THE LEGENDARY JOKE...? A JOKE THAT ONLY A LEGENDARY POKÉMON KNOWS...?

Quiz answer for page 109.

2

ON A JOURNEY FILLED WITH LAUGHTER AND TEARS...?
DO YOU NEED A TISSUE?
SNIFF!
I'M NOT CRY-ING...
I just got something in my eye...

Meowth is a Normal-type Pokémon.

POKÉMON
QUIZ

What category of Pokémon is Meowth?

1 Scratch Cat Pokémon

2 Catty Pokémon

3 Classy Cat Pokémon

tinng
TO MEOWTH'S EYES, OSHAWOTT AND WHISMUR HAVE A RADIANT SHINE TO THEM.

NOTE
THE GOLD COIN ON MEOWTH'S HEAD GLOWS WHEN IT DISCOVERS SOMETHING SHINY.
ting
I'VE FOUND MY NEWS STORY!!
WE'RE GOING TO DO UP-CLOSE-AND-PERSONAL INTERVIEWS WITH THESE TWO!!
UM... THE GLARE IS TOO MUCH FOR THE CAMERA.

MINI-BREAK

3

Beartic

TONGUE TWISTER
A BARE BEARTIC BEARING UNBEARABLE BRRRS.
HMPH
NOTE
BEARTIC USUALLY WALKS ON ALL FOURS.

Quiz answer for page 111.

1

Meowth is a Scratch Cat Pokémon.

Which Pokémon?

Which Pokémon on the right matches which description on the left? See if you can connect them all!

Bully of the Sea	
Beautifly of the Sea	
Guardian of the Sea	
Gem of the Sea	

MINI-BREAK 3

Slowbro

tinng

DON'T LOOK NOW, BUT...
DON'T LOOK NOW, BUT...
smak
flap flap
HUH ?!

Quiz answer for page 113.

?

The answer is on page 253.

MINI-
BREAK
3

DON'T LOOK NOW, BUT ...?
BUT WHAT? BUT WHAT?!
WHAT ARE YOU TALKING ABOUT?

I TOLD YOU... YOUR BUTT.
NOTE
SLOWBRO HAS A SHELLDER CLAMPED ONTO ITS TAIL.
OH, HAT...

MINI-BREAK 3

Larvitar

IT'S A "LARVITARLY" DAY OUT!

NOTE
LARVITAR IS BORN UNDERGROUND. IT EATS THE SOIL AROUND IT BEFORE EMERGING INTO THE AIR.

Which Pokémon?

Which Pokémon on the right matches which category on the left? See if you can connect them all!

Ruffian Pokémon

Irate Pokémon

Hostile Pokémon

Brutal Pokémon

The Legendary Pokémon Terrakion

...WE'VE FINALLY CAUGHT UP...
AND SO...
...WITH TERRA-KION!!

Quiz answer for page 117.
?

ARE YOU A LEGENDARY POKÉMON?
'SCUSE US, BUT...

The answer is on page 254.

POKÉMON
QUIZ

I AM TERRAKION, A LEGENDARY POKÉMON.
YES.

Terrakion uses Rock Slide. Which Pokémon is this super effective against?

Scrafty

Palpitoad

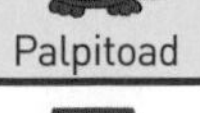

Tranquill

DO YOU KNOW THE LEGENDARY JOKE?!
OUT WITH IT!
WELL...? WHAT...?

The Legendary Joke

IF I, A LEGENDARY POKÉMON, KNOW A JOKE...
...DOES THAT MAKE IT A LEGENDARY JOKE?

Quiz answer for page 119.

3

EXACTLY!! THAT WOULD BE A LEGENDARY JOKE!!
THEN LISTEN CLOSELY...!
OKAY ...
Finally!

Rock Slide is a Rock-type move and would be super effective against Tranquill, who is a Normal- and Flying-type Pokémon.

HEY...
ARE YOU GETTING THIS ON FILM?!
nod

I...

POKéMON QUIZ

Kyogre and Groudon are both Legendary Pokémon. Which one is taller?

1

Kyogre

2

Groudon

3

Neither

Terrakion's Joke

Quiz answer for page 121.

1

Kyogre is 14'09" and Groudon is 11'06", so Kyogre is taller.

I ATE SOME DIRT TODAY...
...AND IT MADE ME TERRA BLY SICK...
URRRGGF...

ch-chirrp
ch-chirrp...
NOT REMOTELY FUNNY...
END OF PART 1

THE QUEST CONTINUES!

PART 2

WILL
OSHAWOTT
AND WHISMUR
FIND THE RIGHT
LEGENDARY
POKÉMON?
AND THE
LEGENDARY
JOKE?

Auditions for the Legendary Joke

LEGENDARY JOKE WANTED!
GOOD EVENING, EVERY-BODY! MEOWTH HERE!!
WE'RE AUDITIONING FOR... THE LEGENDARY JOKE!
Shing
OUR FIRST CHALLENGER IS... DA-DAAH! ♪

POKÉMON
QUIZ

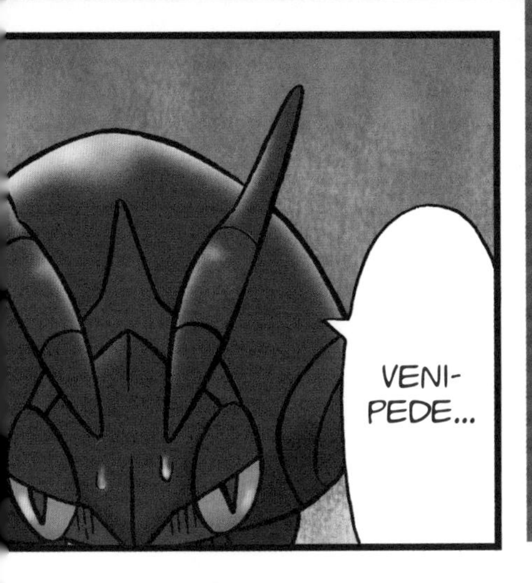
VENI-
PEDE...

I JUST
FLEW IN
FROM
UNOVA,
AND BOY
ARE MY
ARMS
TIRED.
gong
FIRST,
YOU
DON'T
HAVE
ARMS.
SECOND,
THE EXIT
IS THAT
WAY.
int
NOTE
VENIPEDE IS A
VERY AGGRESSIVE
POKÉMON.

Venipede fights its prey by...

1. ...crushing them.
2. ...biting them.
3. ...spitting poison at them.

A Star Is Born?

I'M GOOD AT SINGING...
...AND ACTING AND...

Quiz answer for page 127.

2

ER, EXCUSE ME...?
WHAT ARE YOU TALKING ABOUT ...?
...SIGNING AUTO-GRAPHS AND...

Venipede bites its enemies to poison them.

AND I'M A STAR! JAZZ HANDS !!
I'M SNIVY!

NEXT!!
WANT ME TO SIGN A CON-TRACT NOW?

NOTE

SNIVY'S MOVEMENTS BECOME SWIFTER WHEN IT IS EXPOSED TO SUNLIGHT.

POKÉMON QUIZ

Which part of its body does Snivy use to photo-synthesize?

1 Face

2 Back

3 Tail

Do the Recycle

RECY-CLING GOES IN BLUE BAGS.
GARBAGE GOES IN BROWN BAGS.

Quiz answer for page 129.

3

RECYCLE
BE CAREFUL NOT TO...
...MIX THEM UP WHEN YOU SET THEM ON THE CURB!
GARBAGE
RECYCLING

Snivy photosynthesizes by bathing its tail in sunlight.

POKéMON
QUIZ

BUT WHEN YOU EAT THEM, YOU CAN MIX AND MATCH HOWEVER YOU LIKE!
gulp
Ick!
When you eat them?!

What does Garbodor do in battle after clenching its opponent with its left arm?

1
Squirts poison out of the fingertip of its right arm

2
Belches poison gas from its mouth

3
Crushes it with its left arm

HOW'D I DO?
DON'T CALL US...
...we'll call you.
NOTE
GARBODOR CONSUMES GARBAGE TO CREATE POISON GASES AND LIQUIDS INSIDE ITS BODY.

Something Amazing

WANNA SEE SOMETHING AMAZING?!
HERE GOES!

Quiz answer for page 131.

2

NOTE
ZORUA CAN TRANSFORM ITSELF INTO OTHER PEOPLE AND POKÉMON.
POOF

Garbodor finishes off its opponent by belching poison gas from its mouth.

ta-dah
I'VE TRANSFORMED INTO GIRATINA!
...

YOU DON'T SEEM ALL THAT IMPRESSED.
UM...
ELL... E'RE INDA OOK-ING OR A OKE... NOT AGIC RICKS.

POKÉMON QUIZ

What does Zorua often transform into?

1. Zoroark
2. Giratina
3. A silent child

Grand Illusion

I'M ZOROARK.
AND NOW FOR... A MAGIC TRICK.
NOTHING UP MY SLEEVE...

I WONDER IF ZOROARK REALIZES...
...IT DOESN'T *HAVE* SLEEVES...

Quiz answer for page 133.

3

Zorua often transforms into a child who doesn't talk.

POKÉMON
QUIZ

shff
TA-DA!
plop

Which of the following is not true of Zoroark?

1. It has a strong bond with other members of its pack.
2. It is able to deceive a large group at the same time.
3. It transforms into a silent child.

A TRANQUILL APPEARED FROM INSIDE MY HAT!
Hi!
BUT IT WAS UNDER YOUR HAT THE WHOLE TIME!

Invisible Joke

A MIMED WALL

Quiz answer for page 135.

3

It is Zorua who transforms into a silent child.

MIME?! SERIOUSLY ?!
NOTE
MR. MIME IS A MASTER OF PANTOMIME.
Aak
We're looking for a joke!

WHAT ARE YOU DOING?!
Shfffff!

POKéMON QUIZ

What does Mr. Mime do if its pantomime is interrupted?

1. Uses DoubleSlap on the offender
2. Repeats the pantomime endlessly
3. Gives up and goes home

Hmfff...
Hmfff...
...MIMED JOKE OUT OF A MIMED BAG?!
YOU'RE GOING TO PULL A...

Invisible Joke, II

WHAT ...?
ONE MORE TRY...?
Okay. Last chance ...

Quiz answer for page 137.

1

A TUG-OF-WAR?
Hmfff ...
Hmfff ...

Mr. Mime gets mad and uses DoubleSlap.

Hmmmf
drag
drag

yank
And don't come back...!

Wailord and Snorlax challenge each other in a tug-of-war. The heavier Pokémon will win, so which one does?

1

Wailord

2

Snorlax

3

It's a draw because they weigh the same.

Dance Like Somebody Is Watching You

I'M MELOETTA, CON-TESTANT NUMBER 10!
I'M GOING TO DANCE FOR YOU! ♡

Quiz answer for page 139.

2

Snorlax is heavier, so it wins.

POKÉMON
QUIZ

YOU WIN...♡

...
WAIT! WE'RE ASKING YOU TO MAKE US LAUGH!!
That was close...
But my dances aren't funny. They're interpretative.

Meloetta's melodies make other Pokémon...

1. ...angry.
2. ...sleepy.
3. ...happy or sad.

Something Special

HAVE I GOT SOMETHING SPECIAL FOR YOU! READY ...?♡
OKAY, WAIT FOR IT...

Quiz answer for page 141.

3

HRRMMM...
trmbl trmbl

Meloetta's melodies can make other Pokémon feel happy or sad.

POP POP POP

POKéMON
QUIZ

Genesect is a Pokémon from how many millions of years ago?

1. 100
2. 300
3. 500

WELL? WHAT D'YOU THINK?!
You like it? Huh?
UM... HAPPY NEW YEAR TO YOU TOO...?

Legendary Yoga

OMMM
...

Quiz answer for page 143.

2

OMMM
...

Genesect has been around for 300 million years.

OMMM
...
...
grr

OKAY...
I KNOW A LOT
OF PEOPLE...
...THINK
YOGA
POSES
LOOK
FUNNY...
...but
they
just look
painful
to me!
...
JUDGE

POKÉMON
QUIZ

What unique thing can Medicham see by focusing its mind?

1. Its opponent's aura
2. Tomorrow's weather
3. Things in the distance

The Legendary Island

SORRY, OSHA-WOTT...
I THOUGHT HOLDING AN AUDITION WOULD ATTRACT TALENT, BUT...
We've got nothing.
THAT'S OKAY.

Quiz answer for page 145.
1

Medicham can see the aura of its opponents.

IT'S NOT LIKE WE HAD ANY BETTER IDEAS.
HEY, OSHA-WOTT!

I FOUND A CLUE!
THERE'S A PLACE CALLED LEGENDARY ISLAND!!

AND GUESS WHO LIVES THERE...? THE LEGENDARY POKÉMON ZEKROM AND RESHIRAM!

POKÉMON QUIZ

What is the scalchop on Oshawott's stomach made of?

1. The same substance as its fangs
2. The same substance as its claws
3. Iron

The Quest Continues...

TIME TO SET OUT ON OUR JOURNEY AGAIN!

Quiz answer for page 147.
2

TO REACH LEGENDARY ISLAND WE HAVE TO GO DOWN THIS RIVER...
...AND OVER THIS OCEAN...

Oshawott's scalchop is made from the same material as its claws.

POKéMON
QUIZ

RIVERS ARE FULL OF ALL KINDS OF NASTY THINGS!
BE CAREFUL, EVERY-ONE!

Which of the following Pokémon are immune to Electric-type moves?

1

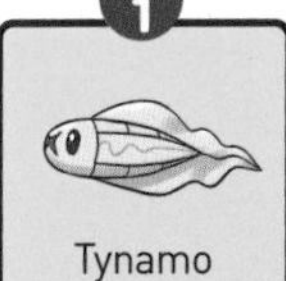

Tynamo

2

Tirtouga

3

Palpitoad

I BET THERE'S A DANGEROUS POKÉMON...
SPLOOSH...
...LURKING UNDER THIS WATER RIGHT NOW!
WAGH! DON'T SCARE ME LIKE THAT!

Gonna Getcha!

OSHAWOTT, WHERE'S YOUR BAG?

HUH?!

OH NO! DID I DROP IT SOMEWHERE?!

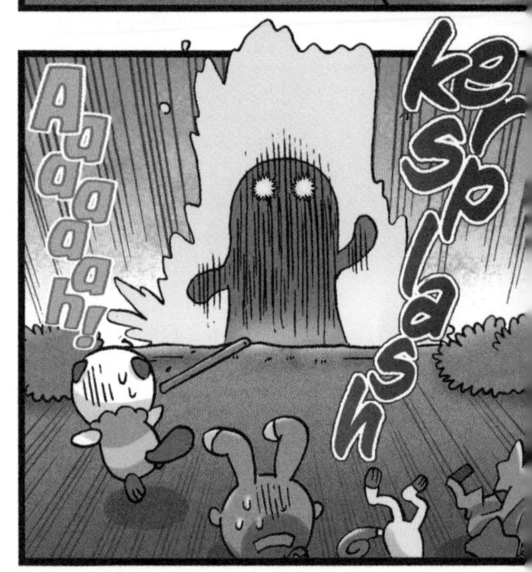

kersplash
Aaaaah!

Quiz answer for page 149.
3

Palpitoad is a Water- and Ground-type Pokémon, so Electric-type moves have no effect upon it.

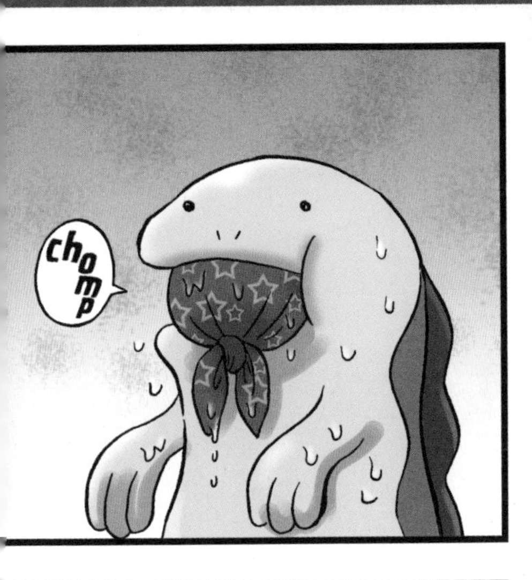
chomp

POKÉMON
QUIZ

Which of the following moves are ineffective against Quagsire?

LOOKING FOR THIS?
WHY, Y-YES... TH-THANK YOU...
TALK ABOUT A SPLASHY ENTRANCE!
NOTE
QUAGSIRE HUNTS BY LEAVING ITS MOUTH WIDE OPEN IN HOPES OF ITS PREY DROPPING INSIDE.

1. Electric-type

2. Flying-type

3. Ground-type

A Little Help

I JUMPED SO HIGH WITH FRIGHT THAT I PUT MY BACK OUT!
OWWW...

Quiz answer for page 151.
1

splish
!

Quagsire is a Water- and Ground-type Pokémon, so Electric-type moves are ineffective against it.

POKéMON
QUIZ

MUDKIP OFFERED TO GIVE YOU A RIDE...
NOTE
MUDKIP IS STRONG ENOUGH TO CARRY A LARGE BOULDER.
HOLD IT RIGHT THERE!
Shff
WHOA! A BANDIT ?!

Mudkip breathes through the gills on its cheeks. Where does it rest?

1. Behind an underwater rock
2. Under the mud on the river bottom
3. In an underwater sinkhole

Master Swordsman

Quiz answer for page 153.

2

Mudkip slathers itself with mud and rests on the bottom of the river.

IT CAN'T BE EASY CARRYING AN INJURED COMRADE...

GIMME A SECOND!

NOTE

PAWNIARD'S BODY IS COMPOSED OF BLADES. IT SHARPENS THEM ON STONES BY THE RIVER.

Chop
Chop

THERE YOU GO!
ta-dah
WOW!
Oooh!
NOW YOU CAN FLOAT DOWN THE RIVER TOGETHER ON THIS RAFT.

SO MANY NICE POKÉ-MON...
...LIVE ALONG THIS RIVER!
I TOLD YOU WE'D BE FINE, WHISMUR!
Thanks!

POKÉMON QUIZ

Pawniard's body is composed of blades. What category of Pokémon is it?

1. Sharp Blade Pokémon
2. Sword Pokémon
3. Royal Sword Pokémon

MINI-BREAK 4

Plusle

A DAY LIKE THIS...
...IS POSITIVELY WONDERFUL!
NOTE
PLUSLE SCATTERS SPARKS FROM ITS BODY WHEN IT CHEERS ITS FRIENDS ON.

Quiz answer for page 155.
1

HEY, ARE YOU ASLEEP?!
NOPE.
I'M CHECKING MY EYELIDS FOR PIN-HOLES.

Pawniard is a Sharp Blade Pokémon.

MINI-
BREAK
4

BUT SERIOUSLY... I'M DROOLING TO WATER THIS SPROUT.
plip

POOR TIRED MINUN...
plip
Is it working ...?
I don't think you have a green thumb.
NOTE
MINUN GIVES OFF SPARKS FROM ITS BODY WHEN ITS PARTNER IS IN JEOPARDY.

MINI-BREAK 4

Gibble

THE MYSTERY DEEPENS!
NOTE
GIBLE USED TO LIVE IN THE TROPICS.
Hmm...
A
B

Whose Head?

Which Pokémon on the right matches which head on the left? See if you can connect them all!

Karrablast

Roggenrola

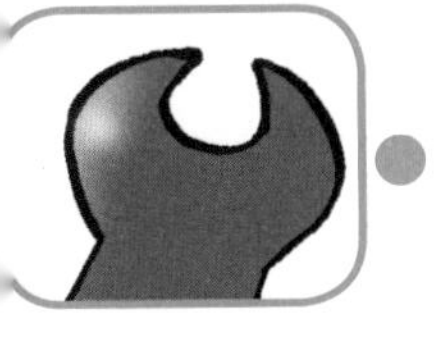

Ducklett

Sigilyph

MINI-BREAK 4

Espeon

Quiz answer for page 159.

?

The answer is on page 254.

ESPEON SENSES IT'S A GREAT DAY TO START A JOURNEY.
BON VOY-AGE...
NOTE
ESPEON CAN PREDICT BOTH ITS ENEMY'S MOVES AND THE WEATHER BY READING AIR CURRENTS.

I KNEW I SHOULD HAVE TAKEN THAT LEFT TURN AT...
WHERE AM I ?!
NOTE
EMOLGA GLIDES BY USING ITS OUTSTRETCHED SKIN AS A SAIL.

MINI-BREAK 4

Emolga

MINI-
BREAK
4

Carvanha

I WISH...
...THAT BERRY WOULD FALL DOWN...
spl
ish
spl
ish

plop
boing

Nuts!
boink
STUPID UNDER-BITE...
NOTE
CARVANHA HAS A STRONGLY DEVELOPED JAW.

MINI-BREAK
4

A Bad Feeling

I DON'T LIKE THIS! I REALLY DON'T LIKE THIS!
WHAT'S NOT TO LIKE?

I DON'T TRUST THIS RIVER!
RELAX, WHISMUR.
YOU WORRY TOO MUCH.

BUT THEN, ALL OF A SUDDEN...
SEE? EVERYTHING'S PERFECTLY FINE.

CELEBI APPEARS BEFORE THEM!
HI THERE. ♡
NOTE
CELEBI HAS THE POWER TO TRAVEL ACROSS TIME. IT IS SAID TO APPEAR ONLY DURING TIMES OF PEACE.

POKéMON QUIZ

What is Celebi the guardian of?

1. Time
2. Fields
3. Forests

Heads Up!

ARE YOU READY?
READY...? FOR WHAT?!

Quiz answer for page 165.
3

I'M A TIME TRAVELER...
SO I CAN TELL YOU...
...WHAT'S COMING UP NEXT.

Celebi is known as a guardian of the forest.

POKéMON
QUIZ

MEANING...?
A WATER-FALL!

NOW YOU TELL US!
OOPS. SORRY... ♡
ker-Splaash

Which of the following is Celebi's Ability?

1. Natural Cure
2. Prankster
3. Marvel Scale

Second Chance

HI AGAIN. FOR THE FIRST TIME. OR SECOND...
YOU'RE IN DANGER!
blip
CELEBI RETURNED TO THREE PAGES AGO.

Quiz answer for page 167.

1

THERE'S A WATER-FALL UP AHEAD.
WHAT...?!
I KNEW IT! ABAN-DON RAFT, ABAN-DON RAFT!

Celebi's Ability is Natural Cure.

THANKS! YOU SAVED US!
WELL, IN THE PAST, YOU ASKED ME TO SAVE YOU IN THE FUTURE...UM...NOW.

POKÉMON QUIZ

What did Celebi bring from the future and leave behind in the forest?

1 Hope

2 Victory

3 An Egg

FALLING ROCK.
krash
ARE YOU KID-DING ME?!
splish
splish
splish

Third Time's the Charm

CELEBI RETURNED TO 15 PAGES AGO.
...AND SO... YOU SHOULDN'T GET ON THAT RAFT!
WHAT ?!
But I went through all this trouble to build it!

Quiz answer for page 169.
3

Celebi brought an egg from the future.

HEY, IF YOU CAN TRAVEL TO THE FUTURE...
...CAN YOU CHECK TO SEE...
...IF WE EVER FIND THE LEGEND-ARY JOKE?

NO TIME! SORRY!
WHICH I REALIZE IS A WEIRD THING FOR A TIME TRAVELER TO SAY...
shing

DON'T WORRY. YOU'LL FIND OUT FOR YOUR-SELVES.
DON'T GIVE UP!

POKÉMON
QUIZ

Celebi is a Guardian of the Forest. What category is it?

1

Mysterious Pokémon

2

Aurora Pokémon

3

Time Travel Pokémon

Told You...

Quiz answer for page 171.

3

OKAY THEN... THANKS, CELEBI!
YOU'VE GIVEN US HOPE...
WE'LL FIND OUT FOR OURSELVES ...?

WHAT NOW?!
SO...
ARE YOU GETTING ON MY RAFT OR NOT?!

Celebi is a Time Travel Pokémon.

kersplash
Aaaaaah!

WELL... THEY FOUND OUT FOR THEM-SELVES...
I TOLD THEM NOT TO TAKE THAT RAFT.
blip
blip
blip

POKÉMON QUIZ

Pawniard is a Sharp Blade Pokémon. Under whose command does it fight?

1

Druddigon

2

Bisharp

3

Gigalith

The Boss of the Legendary... Pirate?!

THE MOST FEARSOME PIRATE OF THEM ALL!!
HEH HEH HEH... I'M HONCH-KROW!

Quiz answer for page 173.

2

...WE CAN ESCAPE INTO THE SKY—IN THE EVENT OF A SUDDEN STORM OR TSUNAMI.
AND WITH THESE WINGS...
fwappa

Pawniard fights at Bisharp's command.

WE CAN FLY OVER THE RAIN CLOUDS...
...AND RETURN AFTER THEY'VE GONE.

SO WE DON'T NEED A PIRATE SHIP. THIS LOG IS MORE THAN ENOUGH!
BUT A SHIP WOULD BE NICE...
float
float

POKéMON
QUIZ

Which Pokémon gather when Honchkrow utters its deep cry?

1

Haunter

2

Shuppet

3

Murkrow

All Hands on Deck!

AHOY, MATEYS! HARD TO STAR-BOARD!
RAISE THE SAILS!

Quiz answer for page 175.

3

FLAP FLAP

Honchkrow is known as the Summoner of Night because it calls Murkrow to gather together.

SAIL
SAIL
SAIL
flap
flap

POKéMON
QUIZ

What does Murkrow like to collect?

1

Shiny objects

2

Sharp objects

3

Round objects

WOULDN'T IT BE FASTER IF WE JUST FLEW...?
WIND
hwoosh— ...

The Ghost Ship

HEY, YOU GUYS...
HAVE YOU EVER SEEN THE GHOST SHIP?
THE... WHAT?!

Quiz answer for page 177.
1

WITHOUT A SOUND, IT APPEARS AT NIGHT...
...AND ABSORBS THE SOULS OF THOSE WHO GAZE UPON IT.

Murkrow is attracted to shiny things.

Pokémon
QUIZ

Seeing a Murkrow at a certain time of day is said to bring misfortune. When?

1 Morning

2 Noon

3 Night

Aaah!
Eek!
Scary!

IS THAT WHY WE DON'T SAIL AT NIGHT?
EXACTLY.
BUT WE'RE SAFE DURING THE DAY, RIGHT? RIGHT?!

The Rival

AHOY, HONCHKROW! YOU'RE STILL USING THAT LOG AS...
...YOUR SO-CALLED SHIP?
The Krookodile
GRR! NOW THERE'S SOMEONE I DIDN'T WANT TO RUN INTO...

Quiz answer for page 179.

3

YOU DON'T HAVE A SHIP EITHER! THAT'S JUST A DINGHY!
OH YEAH?!
The Krookodile
WELL, AT LEAST IT HAS AN ENGINE!

Some believe that seeing a Murkrow at night heralds misfortune.

POKéMON
QUIZ

Krookodile is famous for its unique eyes. What do they allow Krookodile to do?

1 It can see at a great distance.

2 It can see through walls.

3 Its stare can put others to sleep.

FIRST MATE GOLDUCK... IF YOU PLEASE...
AYE AYE, CAP'N!

Yarr arrr!
Told ya!
Splash
Splash
Splash
Splash
I REALLY HATE THAT POKÉ-MON...
NOTE
GOLDUCK IS THE FASTEST POKÉMON SWIMMER.

On the Ocean with Oshawott

BOSS!
ANOTHER SHIP IS APPROACHING US!
WHAT ?!

Quiz answer for page 181.
1

Krookodile's eyes enable it to see far away as if it were using binoculars.

OSHAWOTT AND ITS FRIENDS HAVE REPAIRED THEIR RAFT AND SET OUT TO SEA.
HMM...

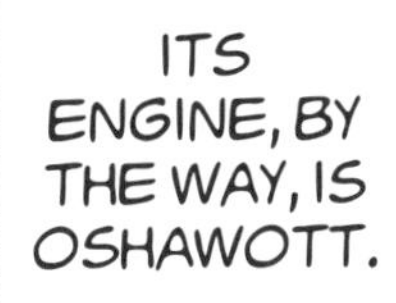
ITS ENGINE, BY THE WAY, IS OSHAWOTT.

splash
splash
splash
SINCE WHEN IS MEOWTH IN CHARGE ?!
SURE!
CAN I TAKE A BREAK?

LET'S STEAL THEIR SHIP! ♡
Heh heh heh heh heh
LOOK AT THOSE FOOLS!

POKéMON QUIZ

Honchkrow uses its Murkrow cronies to...

1 ...warm it.

2 ...surprise others.

3 ...gather food.

Speed Up!

FORTUN-
ATELY,
OSHAWOTT
HAS...

...GROWN
STRONGE
OVER THE
COURSE
OF THEIR
STRENUOU
JOURNEY.

Nice work!

Phew!

Quiz answer for page 183.

3

OSHA-
WOTT
LEARNED
SURF!
HEY,
YOU!
HAND
OVER
YOUR
SHIP!

Honchkrow gets its Murkrow cronies to feed it.

Which of the following Pokémon can learn Surf?

SURF!
KWA-SPLOOSH
AHHH!

AND SO OSHA-WOTT AND FRIENDS...
...SAFELY (AND QUICKLY) REACH LEGENDARY ISLAND.
LEGENDARY ISLAND
WHZZZZZ

1

Watchog

2

Herdier

3

Tranquill

No More Pirate's Life for Me

LET'S STOP BEING PIRATES.
Plip
YEAH ...?
BOSS ...?
Plip
Plip

Quiz answer for page 185.
2

OKAY...
I HAVE A BETTER CAREER FOR YOU ANYWAY...
Gwa ha ha
GIVING UP THE PIRATE LIFE, EH?
Ha ha ha
The Krookodile

Although Herdier is a Normal-type Pokémon, it can learn Surf.

POKéMON
QUIZ

A BETTER CAREER, HUH...?
AND WHAT WOULD THAT BE?

FASTER, MY ENGINES! ♡
Har har har
splash splash
The Krookodile

Which part of Krookodile is strong enough to crush an automobile? Its...

1 ...teeth.

2 ...jaws.

3 ...claws.

MINI-
BREAK
5

Treecko

Bifff

Quiz answer for page 187.

2

pat
pat
pat

Krookodile's jaws are extremely powerful.

MINI-BREAK

5

I MEANT TO DO THAT...
KOFF KOFF
(SURE IT DID...)
NOTE
TREECKO FIGHTS BY STRIKING ITS ENEMIES WITH ITS TAIL.

MINI-
BREAK
5

Gyarados

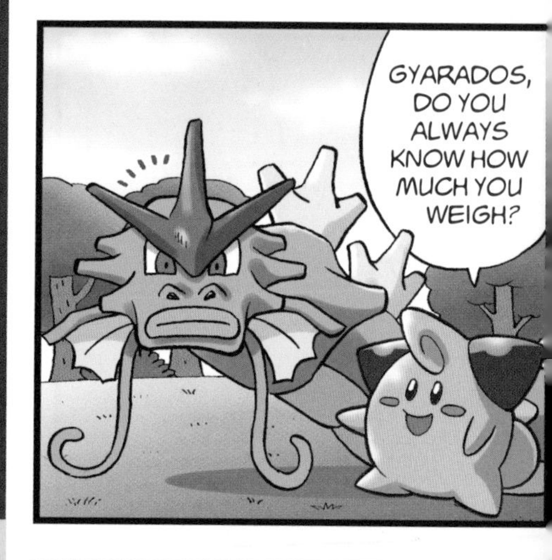
GYARADOS, DO YOU ALWAYS KNOW HOW MUCH YOU WEIGH?

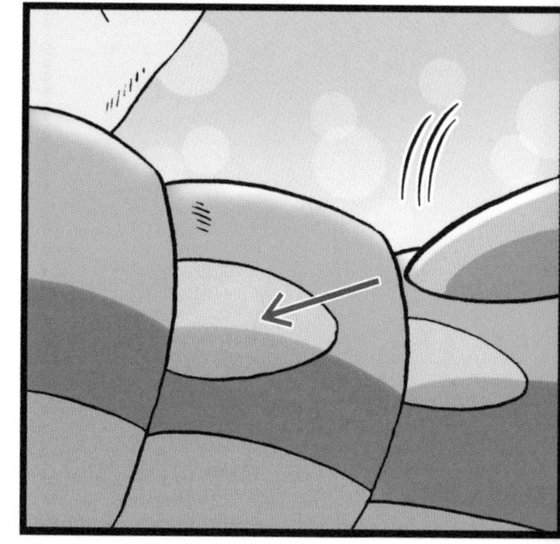

IT'S NOT THAT KIND OF SCALE!
NOTE
WHEN GYARADOS GOES ON A RAMPAGE, IT DOESN'T STOP.

MINI-BREAK 5

MINI-BREAK 5

Shinx

SHINX NEVER SHRINKS FROM EATING BERRIES.
NOTE
ITS FUR SHINES WHEN IT SENSES DANGER.

MARILL WANTS TO SKIP ROPE...
NOTE
MARILL'S FUR NATURALLY REPELS WATER.
SQUITCH
...BUT SERPERIOR DOESN'T WANT TO PLAY.
NOTE
SERPERIOR RAISES ITS HEAD TO INTIMIDATE ITS OPPONENTS.

MINI-BREAK 5

Marill

MINI-
BREAK
5

Munchlax

MUNCHLAX NEVER MET A SNACK IT DIDN'T LIKE.
NOTE
MUNCHLAX HIDES FOOD UNDER ITS LONG BODY FUR.

MINI-
BREAK

5

Which Pokémon?

Which Pokémon on the right matches which category on the left? See if you can connect them all!

Rogue Pokémon

Savage Pokémon

Hostile Pokémon

Brutal Pokémon

Welcoming Committee

SO THIS IS LEG-ENDARY ISLAND...
THERE SHOULD BE A RUIN SOMEWHERE AROUND HERE...

Quiz answer for page 195.

?

NOTE
COFAGRIGUS PRETENDS TO BE AN ELABORATE COFFIN TO SCARE GRAVE ROBBERS AND TEACH THEM A LESSON.

The answer is on page 255.

BOO!

I SAID, "BOO!"
HEY!
Oblivious
UM...
DO YOU HEAR SOME-THING?

POKÉMON QUIZ

What does Cofagrigus like to eat?

1. People
2. Souls
3. Gold nuggets

Off-Limits

HOLD IT RIGHT THERE!
YOU MAY NOT CONTINUE ONE STEP FARTHER! THIS PLACE IS OFF-LIMITS!
THERE HAVE BEEN A LOT OF ROBBERS IN THE AREA LATELY, SO I'M GUARDING THIS ISLAND FROM TRESPASSERS.

Quiz answer for page 197.
3

WE JUST CAME TO MEET RESHIRAM AND ZEKROM.
WHERE CAN WE FIND THEM?!

Cofagrigus likes to feed on gold nuggets.

POKÉMON
QUIZ

What is Cofagrigus's body covered in?

1. Pure gold
2. Ancient cloth
3. Stone

BUT EVEN IF I DID, I WOULDN'T TELL YOU!
Wff
I DUNNO ...

I TOLD YOU THIS PLACE IS OFF-LIMITS!
HEY! COME BACK HERE ...!
tmp tmp tmp

Get 'Em!

THAT'S RIGHT! THIS PLACE IS OFF-LIMITS TO ALL!
WE'LL ATTACK ANYONE WHO STEPS INTO THE RUINS!
NOTE
SIGILYPH WAS ONCE THE GUARDIAN OF AN ANCIENT CITY.

Quiz answer for page 199.
1

...SIT INTO THE RUINS?
WHAT IF WE...
UM...
plomp
plomp

Cofagrigus's body is gilded with pure gold.

POKéMON
QUIZ

WHAT IF WE ROLL INTO THE RUINS...?
roll roll roll...
roll

What did Sigilyph do in ancient cities?

1 Build them

2 Watch for invaders

3 Attack enemies

UH...
WELL ...
THEY GOT YA THERE...

Going Down

LOOK, OSHA-WOTT...
STAIRS!
I BET THEY LEAD TO...

Quiz answer for page 201.
2

...A BASE-MENT.

Sigilyph kept watch for invaders of its ancient cities.

WEL-
COME.
I AM
RESHI-
RAM.
WHAT
BRINGS
YOU
HERE?
NOTE
THE WORLD'S WEATHER CHANGES WHEN RESHIRAM'S TAIL IS ABLAZE.

HURRAY!
WE
FINALLY
FOUND
YOU!
PLEASE
TEACH US
THE REAL
LEGENDARY
JOKE!

POKéMON QUIZ

Reshiram is a Legendary Pokémon said to be capable of which of the following?

1. Turning barren land into a field of flowers
2. Scorching the world with fire
3. Growing abundant crops

Now Appearing... Reshiram!

THE REAL LEGEND-ARY JOKE?
VERY WELL...

Quiz answer for page 203.

2

SEE HOW MY BODY...
...IS THE COLOR OF SNOW?

Reshiram is said to have the power to scorch the world with its fire.

POKÉMON
QUIZ

FWIP
THAT MEANS EVERY-THING IS GOING TO BE "ALL WHITE"...

What happens throughout the world when Reshiram's tail shoots flames?

1. General trouble
2. Volcanoes erupt
3. The weather changes

THAT WASN'T FUNNY AT ALL.
...instead of "all right." Get it ...?
groan
Now what ?

And Now... Zekrom!

HEH HEH HEH...
YOUR JOKE WAS TERRIBLE.
AS USUAL.
ZEK-ROM ?!

Quiz answer for page 205.
3

HELLO, EVERYONE...!
Huh...?
What ...?

When Reshiram's tail is aflame, its heat travels through the atmosphere and changes the world's climate.

POKéMON
QUIZ

I'M SHOCKED TO SEE YOU HERE!
ZZZt
ZZZt
ZZZt
ZZZt
NOTE
ZEKROM CREATES ELECTRICITY WITH ITS TAIL.

NO! THAT'S THE KIND OF JOKE THEY'RE LOOKING FOR! ♡
ARE YOU KIDDING ME?!
Ha ha ha...

Legendary Pokémon Zekrom can do which of the following?

1. Scorch the world with lightning
2. Set off month-long storms
3. Create islands

The Laff-Off

Quiz answer for page 207.

1

Zekrom can scorch the world with lightning.

YOUR JOKES REALLY BURN ME UP!
FOOSH
NOTE
FLAME SHOOTS OUT OF RESHIRAM'S TAIL.
Whoa !!

aahhh
Why, you...
aahhh
Smash
aahhh
THEY'VE BEGUN TO FIGHT...!
Smash
Aaaaaah!

SOME-
BODY
HAS TO
STOP
THEM...
...OR THIS
ISLAND
WILL SINK
INTO THE
SEA!
krmbl
krmbl
krmmmbl

I'LL
TAKE
CARE OF
THEM!

POKéMON
QUIZ

What can Kyurem generate inside its body?

1. Fire energy
2. Wind energy
3. Freezing energy

Kyurem Too...

STOP FIGHTING!

Quiz answer for page 209.

3

blop
HUH?
NOTE
KYUREM + ZEKROM = BLACK KYUREM

Kyurem generates a powerful freezing energy.

PERFECT!
HEY! NO FAIR!
KYUREM AND ZEKROM HAVE GONE THROUGH ABSOFUSION!

MWAHAHAHAHA...!
SO BE QUIET, LISTEN CLOSELY AND PREPARE TO LAUGH!
NOW I WILL TELL YOU THE REAL LEGENDARY JOKE!

POKéMON
QUIZ

What is Black Kyurem's Ability?

1. Pressure
2. Turboblaze
3. Teravolt

And Next... Black Kyurem

I'M SHOCKED TO SEE YOU HERE!

THAT'S THE SAME JOKE AS BEFORE!
ARE YOU KIDDING?! IT'S TOTALLY DIFFERENT!

Quiz answer for page 211.

3

Black Kyurem's Ability is Teravolt, which is the same as Zekrom's Ability.

SEE ?!
krik
krek
NOTE
BLACK KYUREM'S MOVE, FREEZE SHOCK, IS AN ICE-TYPE MOVE.
*THEY'RE FROZEN STIFF.

I WANT TO GO THROUGH ABSO-FUSION WITH KYUREM TOO!
oss
slap
HUH?

Which of the following Pokémon is Freeze Shock not very effective against?

1

Whismur

2

Oshawott

3

Scrafty

And Finally... White Kyurem!

Argh!
HEH HEH ...
I LOOK COOL, DON'T I?
NOTE
KYUREM + RESHIRAM = WHITE KYUREM

Quiz answer for page 213.
2

Ice-type moves are not very effective against Water-type Pokémon like Oshawott.

AND NOW FOR MY LEGENDARY JOKE! GUESS WHAT? NOW THAT I'VE BECOME WHITE KYUREM...
...I'M "ALL WHITE." GET IT...?
TAIL

YOU'RE THE ONE REPEATING THE SAME JOKE!
Cut it out, you two!
grrr grrr
Aaargh!
ACK! THEY'RE FIGHTING AGAIN!

JUST THEN, A SHADOWY FORM GALLOPS THROUGH THE FALLING RUBBLE...
krnch
krnch
dash

POKÉMON QUIZ

Which one is taller, White Kyurem or Black Kyurem?

1. White Kyurem
2. Black Kyurem
3. They're both the same height.

MINI-BREAK 6

Farfetch'd

FARFETCH'D USES A GREEN ONION STALK AS A WEAPON!

Quiz answer for page 215.

AT TIMES, IT CAN BE USED TO BUILD A NEST.

White Kyurem is taller.

MINI-BREAK 6

ALSO, IT HELPS ME HUNT!
HUH? IT HELPS YOU... HUNT?

YEP! BY HELPING ME "STALK" MY PREY!
WHY DID I ASK...? GROAN...
KRUNCH

MINI-
BREAK
6

Metapod

A TEPIG
TOTEM POLE
NOTE
METAPOD STAYS MOTION-
LESS IN ITS SHELL WHILE IT
WAITS TO EVOLVE.

Whose Arm?

Which Pokémon on the right matches which arm on the left? See if you can connect them all!

Bisharp

Pansage

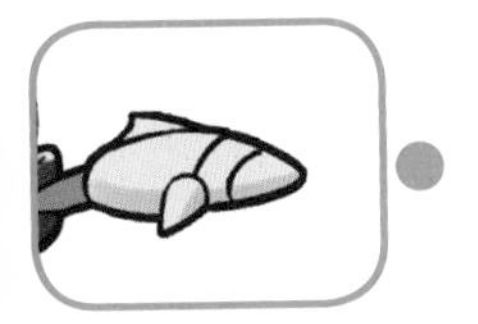

Cofagrigus

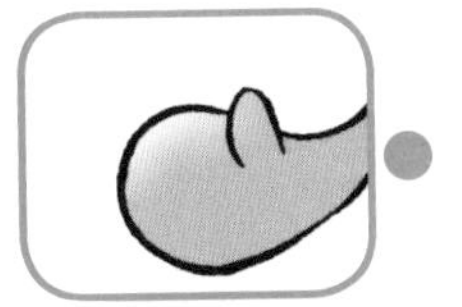

Eelektross

MINI-
BREAK

Zubat

SO YOU'RE MY NEW ASSIS- TANT?
THAT'S RIGHT, SUPER SLEUTH WHISMUR.
NOTE
ZUBAT HAS NO EYES BUT EMITS AN ULTRASONIC SOUND FROM ITS MOUTH TO "SEE" ITS SURROUNDINGS.

Quiz answer for page 219.

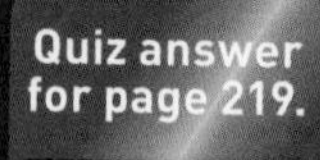

?

NO MATTER HOW DIFFICULT THE CASE MAY BE— I'LL SOLVE IT!
chomp
I NEVER BITE OFF MORE THAN I CAN CHEW!
ZUK ZUK

The answer is on page 255.

UNLIKE MARILL, WHISMUR ISN'T TRYING TO SKIP ROPE (SEE PAGE 193).
QUIT CHOMP-ING ON ME!!
SMAK

YOU'RE FIRED!
AWW... BEING FIRED REALLY BITES...

MINI-BREAK 6

Stunfisk

IF YOU'RE SLEEPY, TAKE A NAP. ♡
NOTE
STUNFISK PARALYZES ITS PREY WITH JOLTS OF ELECTRICITY GENERATED FROM ITS BODY.
ZZZ
ZZZ
ZZZ
STUNFISK'S ELECTRIC BLANKET

YOU KNOW YOU'RE SUPPOSED TO PLUG IT INTO AN ELECTRICAL OUTLET, RIGHT?

MINI-BREAK 6

Cubchoo

I'M TRYING SNOT TO CRY SO MUCH...
NOTE
CUBCHOO'S SNOT IS STICKY WHEN IT'S HEALTHY.

Keldeo to the Rescue!

SUDDENLY KELDEO APPEARS!
HURRY!
I'LL SHOW YOU THE WAY OUT!
NOTE
KELDEO'S ABILITY IS JUSTIFIED.

RMBL
RMBL
RMBL

hff
hff
hff
YOU'RE SAFE NOW!

THAT WAS A CLOSE CALL!
IT'S ALWAYS LIKE THIS WHEN THOSE THREE GET TOGETHER...

POKÉMON
QUIZ

Where does Keldeo usually appear?

1. Deep in the forest
2. At waterfronts
3. On the peak of steep mountains

The Return of Celebi!

Fliff
CELEBI?!
CELEBI ASKED ME TO HELP YOU OUT.
YOU REALLY OUGHT TO BE MORE CARE-FUL!

Quiz answer for page 225.

2

I COULDN'T FORGET ABOUT YOU AND YOUR QUEST...
SO I TRAVELED THROUGH TIME TO SEE WHAT HAPPENED.

Keldeo appears at waterfronts.

I EVEN TRAVELED TO THAT FIRST DAY WHEN IT ALL STARTED...
Poof...
grump grump
I'LL MOON PIKACHU... WITH A LUNAR POKÉMON!

AND I FOUND OUT WHY PIKA-CHU...
...WASN'T SMILING!
YOU DID ?!

POKÉMON QUIZ

What category of Pokémon is Keldeo?

1. Colt Pokémon
2. Jet Pokémon
3. Fairy Pokémon

Pikachu's Secret

Quiz answer for page 227.

1

PIKA-
CHU!
THE REASON IS...

WHERE HAVE YOU BEEN?!
OSHAWOTT!
...

Keldeo is a Colt Pokémon.

POKéMON
QUIZ

hurummph

DOESN'T MATTER... COME WITH ME NOW!

Where does Pikachu live?

1

In a town

2

On top of a mountain

3

In the forest

Birthday Party!

Quiz answer for page 229.

3

Happy Birthday, Oshawott!
I WAS PREPARING A SURPRISE PARTY FOR YOU.
BUT YOUR BIRTH-DAY IS OVER NOW... SIGH...

Pikachu lives in the forest.

SO THAT'S WHY YOU WERE BEING SO WEIRD AND DISTANT!
BECAUSE YOU DIDN'T WANT TO GIVE AWAY THE SURPRISE!
WHERE WERE YOU?!

POKÉMON QUIZ

When Pikachu raises its tail, what is it doing?

1. Checking its surroundings
2. Calling its friends
3. Discharging electricity

...TO GO LOOKING FOR THE LEGENDARY JOKE...IN THE FIRST PLACE...
WHICH MEANS... I NEVER NEEDED...
TOTAL WASTE OF TIME.

The Final Cut

ta-dah
OKAY, EVERY-BODY...
TAKE A LOOK AT THE VIDEO SCREEN!
MEOWTH!

Quiz answer for page 231.
1

blip
...TO FILM OUTTAKES—SCENES THAT MEOWTH MISSED!
I BORROWED THE VIDEO CAMERA...
CELEBI!

Pikachu checks its surroundings when it raises its tail.

OH COOL...!
Can I watch ?!
LET'S WATCH THE FILM FROM THE VERY BEGINNING!

AND REVIEW EVERY JOKE WE FOUND ALONG OUR JOURNEY!
THE END
BUT FIRST...

Watchog's Joke

REC
Huh?
ARE YOU FILMING?

REC
JUST SO YOU KNOW... I'M NOT A THIEF OR ANYTHING!
I'm actually a nice guy!

ANYHOW...
I'VE GOT A HILARIOUS JOKE FOR YOU!
YOU'VE GOT TO FILM IT!

READY?
ook! This is my...
...in-visible hand pup-pet!

Which attack is not effective against Watchog?

1. Shadow Ball
2. Energy Ball
3. Gyro Ball

Virizion and Cobalion's Joke

RE
YOU WANT US TO TELL YOU A JOKE?
I THOUGHT WE TOLD YOU WE'RE NOT GOOD AT THINGS LIKE THAT.

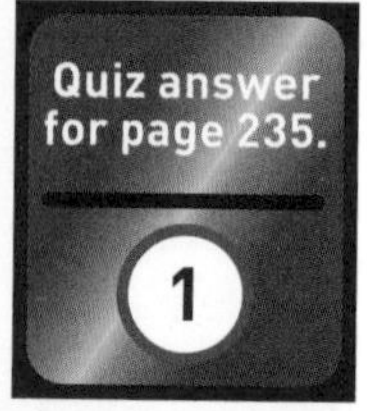

Quiz answer for page 235.
1

Watchog is a Normal-type Pokémon, so Ghost-type moves like Shadow Ball are not effective against it.

PLEASE!
SO MANY POKÉMON ARE LOOKING FORWARD TO THIS FILM...!

WELL, OKAY...
KNOCK KNOCK!
WHAT ARE YOU DOING? THERE'S NO DOOR HERE!

Uh...
Well...
THAT'S THE START OF A JOKE...
YOU MEAN THERE'S SUPPOSED TO BE MORE?

POKÉMON
QUIZ

What category of Pokémon is Virizion?

1

Iron Will Pokémon

2

Leaf Pokémon

3

Grassland Pokémon

Pansage's Joke

REC
PLEASE...
PLEASE!

Quiz answer for page 237.

3

DON'T EVER "LEAF" ME!
PRETTY PLEASE...!
UM...

Virizion is a Grassland Pokémon.

POKÉMON
QUIZ

I DON'T GET THE JOKE, BUT I GOT THE SHOT...

THANKS! ♡
Hey... WHAT DID I JUST SAY?!

What is Pansage's Ability?

1. Chlorophyll
2. Gluttony
3. Overgrow

Terrakion's Joke

...AND IT MADE ME "TERRA-BLY" SICK.
TOO "PUNNY" ?
UMM...
IS THAT ALL YOU'VE GOT?

Quiz answer for page 239.

2

I NEED TO GO...
Urgghh...

Pansage's Ability is Gluttony.

WHY'D YOU HAVE TO SAY YOU "NEED TO GO"?!
smash

TERRAKION HAS BEEN RUNNING ALL OVER THE PLACE EVER SINCE...
Bathroom... Need... bathroom...

POKÉMON QUIZ

What category of Pokémon is Terrakion?

1. Bash Buffalo Pokémon
2. Cavern Pokémon
3. Wild Bull Pokémon

Weavile's Joke...on Pansage

REC
YOU WANT TO KNOW IF I'M GLAD TO HAVE QUIT MY JOB AS A CAMERA OPERATOR...?

Quiz answer for page 241.
2

OF COURSE I AM!
I LOVE BEING THE LEADER OF THIS GROUP! ♡
WOO-HOO
WOO-HOO
WOO-HOO
Our leader! ♡
Our leader! ♡

Terrakion is a Cavern Pokémon.

ta-dah
NOTE
WEAVILE TAKES PRIDE IN ITS CREST TOO.

DOES THIS HERALD A CHANGE IN LEADER-SHIP?
Uh-oh...
murmurmurmur

POKÉMON
QUIZ

In what climate does Weavile live?

1 Hot

2 Cool

3 Cold

Meloetta's Joke... or Prank

REC
JUST KEEP SAYING...
..."CHARMED OVER AND OVER AGAIN!

Quiz answer for page 243.
3

CHARMED CHARMED CHARMED CHARMED CHARMED CHARMED...
Tee-hee...
HUH?

Weavile lives in cold regions.

THAT'S NOT ONE OF MY MOVES, BUT...
...APPAR-ENTLY YOU ARE— BY ME! ♡

ting
SO... CUTE... ♡

POKÉMON
QUIZ

What does Meloetta do to change into its Pirouette Forme during battle?

1. Gets injured
2. Uses Relic Song
3. Uses Rest

Keldeo's Joke

I DON'T KNOW IF I WANT TO TELL A JOKE...
MAYBE I DO... MAYBE I DON'T...

Quiz answer for page 245.

2

IT'S NOT FAIR IF YOU'RE THE ONLY ONE WHO DOESN'T!
YOU HAVE TO TAKE A STAND FOR HUMOR! BE RESOLUTE!
YOU WANT ME TO BE... RESOLUTE?!

Meloetta changes into Pirouette Forme when it uses Relic Song during a battle.

Pokémon
QUIZ

Wom
Wom Wom Wom

ta-dah
DONE!
NOTE
KELDEO CHANGES INTO ITS POWERFUL RESOLUTE FORM WHEN IT FEELS RESOLUTE.

What happens when Keldeo changes into its Resolute Form?

1. It moves faster.
2. It grows larger.
3. It becomes heavier.

Keldeo's Plan

I KNOW!
I'LL GO SHOPPING FOR A JOKE!

Quiz answer for page 247.
1

klop klop

Keldeo moves faster when it changes into its Resolute Form.

WHAT?
I CAN'T BUY A JOKE ANY-WHERE?
klomp klomp
THERE AREN'T ANY STORES IN THE FOREST...

HMPH. WELL, I TRIED!

POKÉMON QUIZ

Which move does Keldeo have to forget to return to its Ordinary Form?

1 Ancient Power

2 Tri Attack

3 Secret Sword

The Legendary Joke... Reel

Haha haha ha
Aha ha ha ha ha
Bwa ha ha ha ha ha
ha ha ha ha

Quiz answer for page 249.

3

Keldeo returns to its Ordinary Form when it forgets Secret Sword.

AFTER THIS VIEWING OF THE FILM, IT WAS BURIED SOME-WHERE. AND THUS THE REAL LEGENDARY JOKE BECAME KNOWN AS...
...THE LEGENDARY JOKE REEL!
THE END... For real!

Thanks for reading all the way to the end!

Quiz on Page 27

MINI-
BREAK
1
Whose Tail?
Which Pokémon on the right
matches which tail on the left?
See if you can connect them all!
(27)

Quiz on Page 31

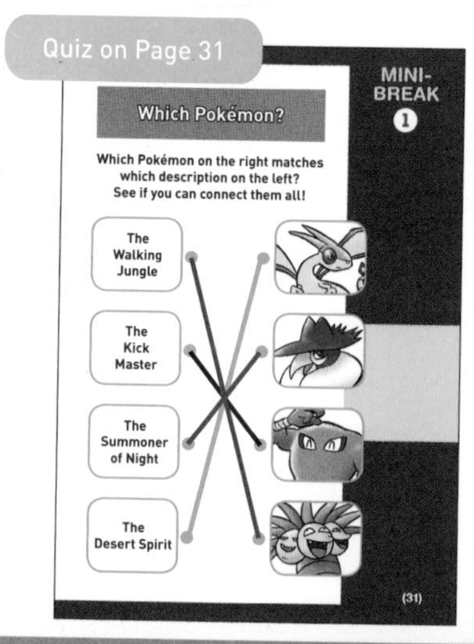

MINI-
BREAK
1
Which Pokémon?
Which Pokémon on the right matches
which description on the left?
See if you can connect them all!
The Walking Jungle
The Kick Master
The Summoner of Night
The Desert Spirit
(31)

Quiz on Page 57

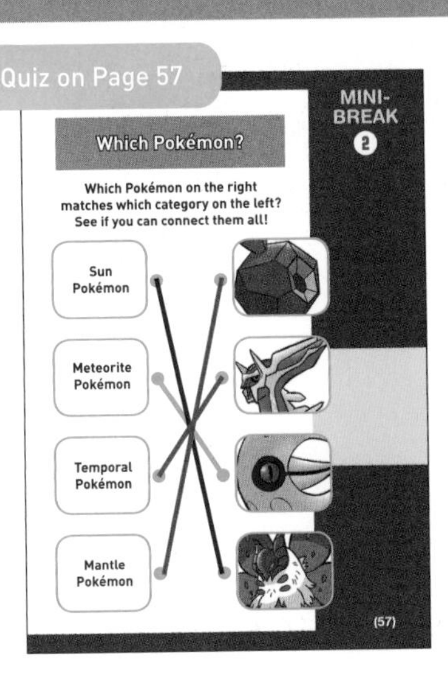

MINI-BREAK 2
Which Pokémon?
Which Pokémon on the right matches which category on the left? See if you can connect them all!
Sun Pokémon
Meteorite Pokémon
Temporal Pokémon
Mantle Pokémon
(57)

Quiz on Page 113

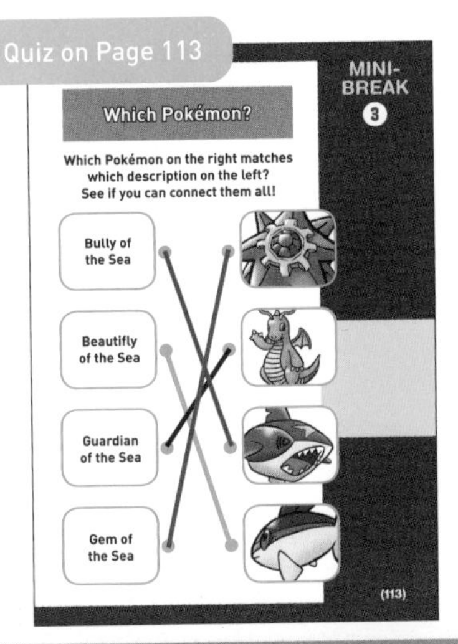

MINI-BREAK 3
Which Pokémon?
Which Pokémon on the right matches which description on the left? See if you can connect them all!
Bully of the Sea
Beautifly of the Sea
Guardian of the Sea
Gem of the Sea
(113)

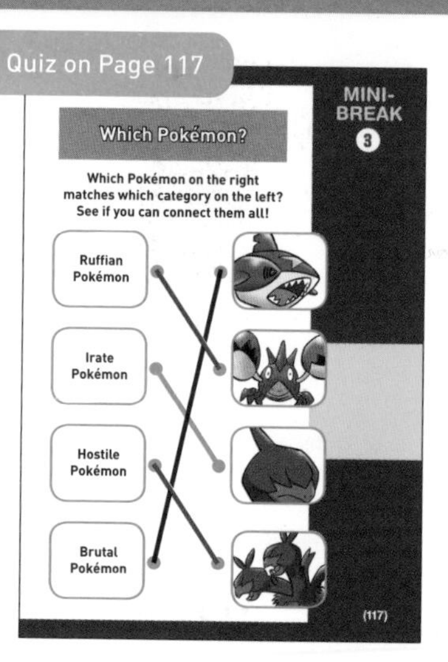
Quiz on Page 117
MINI-BREAK
3
Which Pokémon?
Which Pokémon on the right matches which category on the left? See if you can connect them all!
Ruffian Pokémon
Irate Pokémon
Hostile Pokémon
Brutal Pokémon
(117)

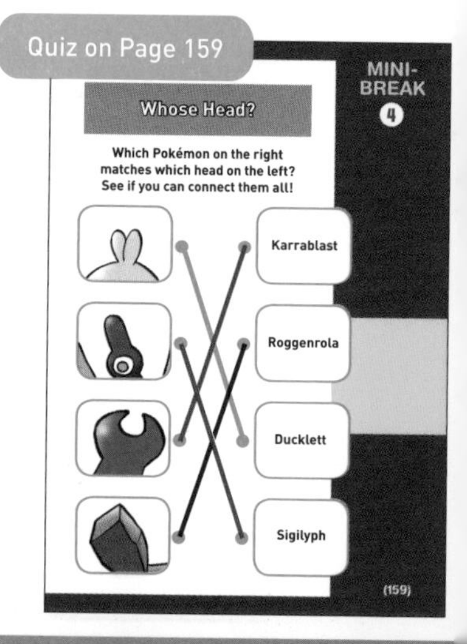
Quiz on Page 159
MINI-BREAK
4
Whose Head?
Which Pokémon on the right matches which head on the left? See if you can connect them all!
Karrablast
Roggenrola
Ducklett
Sigilyph
(159)

Quiz on Page 195

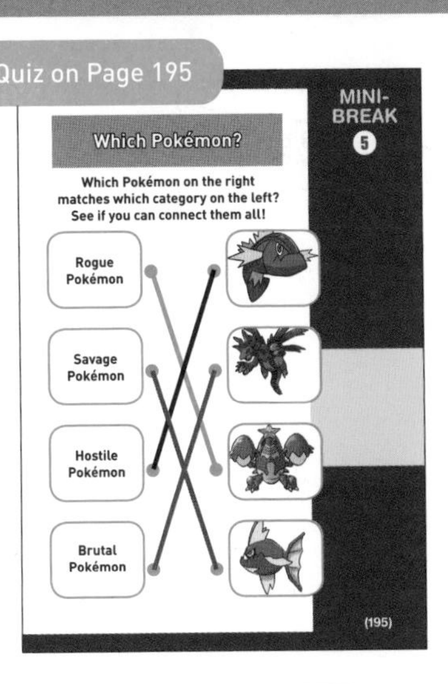

MINI-BREAK 5
Which Pokémon?
Which Pokémon on the right matches which category on the left? See if you can connect them all!
Rogue Pokémon
Savage Pokémon
Hostile Pokémon
Brutal Pokémon
(195)

Quiz on Page 219

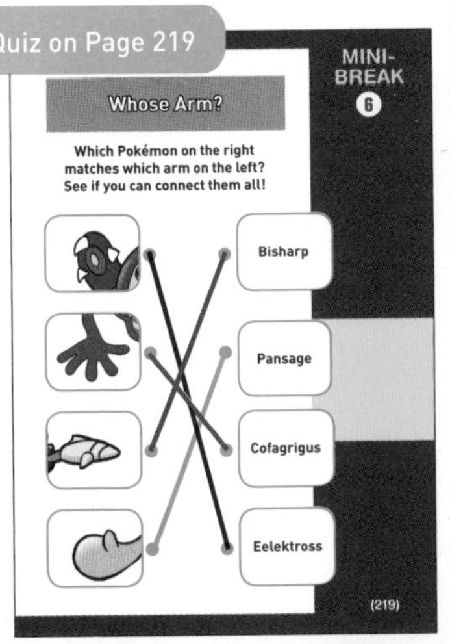

MINI-BREAK 6
Whose Arm?
Which Pokémon on the right matches which arm on the left? See if you can connect them all!
Bisharp
Pansage
Cofagrigus
Eelektross
(219)

Pokémon Pocket Comics
Perfect Square Edition

Story & Art by SANTA HARUKAZE

English Adaptation/Bryant Turnage, Annette Roman
Translation/Tetsuichiro Miyaki
Touch-up & Lettering/Susan Daigle-Leach
Design/Shawn Carrico
Editor/Annette Roman

Printed in China

Published by VIZ Media, LLC
P.O. Box 77010
San Francisco, CA 94107

10 9 8 7 6 5 4 3 2 1
First printing, October 2015

viz
media

PERFECT SQUARE

RATED
A
FOR
ALL AGES
PARENTAL ADVISORY
POKÉMON POCKET COMICS is rated A and is suitable for readers of all ages.
ratings.viz.com